A WILLOWBROOK MIRACLE

The Willowbrook Series
Book 1

By Laura Landon

ARE YOU SIGNED UP FOR DRAGONBLADE'S BLOG?

You'll get the latest news and information on exclusive giveaways, exclusive excerpts, coming releases, sales, free books, cover reveals and more.

Check out our complete list of authors, too!

No spam, no junk. That's a promise!

Sign Up Here

www.dragonbladepublishing.com

Dearest Reader;

Thank you for your support of a small press. At Dragonblade Publishing, we strive to bring you the highest quality Historical Romance from some of the best authors in the business. Without your support, there is no 'us', so we sincerely hope you adore these stories and find some new favorite authors along the way.

Happy Reading!

CEO, Dragonblade Publishing

Additional Dragonblade books by Author Laura Landon

The Willowbrook Series
A Willowbrook Miracle (Book 1)

Men of Valor Series
A Love For All Time (Book 1)
A Love That Knows No Bounds (Book 2)
A Love That's Worth The Risk (Book 3)
A Love That Heals the Heart (Book 4)

CHAPTER ONE

Lady Victoria Crawley closed the book she'd been reading to the Duke of Willowbrook and silently placed it on the bedside table.

"Are you leaving?" the elderly duke asked. His eyes remained closed and his breathing even and slow.

Torie smiled. "I thought you were asleep, Your Grace."

"I know. I can always tell when you think you've lulled me to sleep by the lilt of your sweet voice. Your voice gets softer and softer and you read slower and slower."

"Has anyone ever told you that you are a terrible tease?"

"Yes, you tell me that all the time. Just like your grandmother used to."

"Did you tease her like you tease me?"

"Of course I did. She was almost as fun to tease then as you are now."

"Almost?"

"Yes, almost. But not quite. She didn't realize what I was doing as quickly as you do."

"I'm going to tell her what you said."

The duke's eyes popped open. "No, don't," he pleaded.

"Why ever not?"

"That will hurt her feelings."

"Very well," Torie said, relaxing against her chair. "I won't tell her."

The Duke of Willowbrook settled his head on his pillow. His eyes closed and he appeared more peaceful. "Thank you, Torie. And thank you for coming."

"Of course, Your Grace." Victoria straightened the bottles of medicine and tonics on the table beside the duke's bed. "I'm guessing you loved her, didn't you, Your Grace?"

"Who? Your grandmother?"

"Yes."

He hesitated the briefest of moments. "Yes," he answered softly. "I did."

"Did you ever tell her?"

He smiled. "I didn't have to. Your grandmother knew. But she was happily married to your grandfather and I was happily married to my duchess. There was no sense in talking about something that could never be."

Torie thought how sad that admission was. It had been several years since her grandfather died, and as many years that His Grace had been alone, as well. Perhaps they could have at least offered each other a bit of company over the years. She wondered why they hadn't.

When Torie had everything put away, she reached for the duke's hand and squeezed his fingers. "I need to be going. Grandmama will begin to worry about me."

"Have Jenkins take you home. It's cold out there."

"Not that cold, Your Grace. And I've been sitting all day. It will do me good to walk a bit."

"Did you notice if there were any missives for me on the table?"

"Not that I saw, Your Grace."

"Why do you think Hunter hasn't written? It's been almost a month since I wrote to inform him that his brother has died. I thought he would have sent word that he was returning."

"He'll be home soon, Your Grace. The Crimean Peninsula is far away. And it's difficult to know when he may have received your letter. The post travels ever so slowly during the war."

"You're right, my dear," he said. "I just want him home. I need him back here where I know he'll be safe. With Stephen dead, he's the only remaining heir."

"Don't worry, Your Grace. He'll be here any day now."

"I hope you are right. Have you ever met him, Victoria?"

Torie shook her head. "No, I've not had the pleasure."

"We'll celebrate with a party for him when he returns so everyone can welcome him home."

Torie couldn't help but smile. "Oh, that will be special."

"We'll have to have lots of food and lots of dancing. Hunt was a very good dancer. All the females wanted to dance with him. But that might have been because he was so very good-looking. He cut a fine figure on the dance floor."

"I'm sure he did, Your Grace. He no doubt takes after you." Torie pulled the covers up beneath the duke's chin. "Now, close your eyes and take a short nap before Jenkins brings up your dinner." She reached out and gave the duke's fingers a squeeze.

"What would I do without you, my lady?"

Torie smiled. "I have no idea, Your Grace. You're extremely fortunate that I'm here."

The duke gave a feeble guffaw as Torie left the room. She closed the door behind her and walked to the stairs.

"How is he today?"

Torie looked at the woman climbing the stairs and forced a smile. The duke's nephew, Franklin Ralston, had arrived for the holiday season with his wife, Eulalia, and their son, Connor. Eulalia was nearing Torie on the stairs.

Franklin and Eulalia Ralston insisted that they spend every Christmas season with the duke, even though His Grace never sent them an invitation. Torie's grandmother had hinted that the only reason they came was because His Grace was always generous with his monetary gifts at Christmas.

Grandmama was convinced that all His Grace had to do to discourage the Ralstons from spending Christmas with him was to stop being so generous. But the duke would never do that. He felt guilty because he'd been born first, and Frank's father had been born several years later.

Torie's grandmama said she was just thankful that His Grace still had a grandson alive to stop the Ralstons from being the next in line to inherit the Willowbrook title and estates.

"His Grace seems to be in quite good humor today," Torie said in answer to Eulalia's question. "Christmas has always been his favorite time of the year. And he's especially looking forward to having his grandson home this Christmas."

"And what are *you* hoping for, Lady Victoria?"

Torie was confused by Mrs. Ralston's question. "I'm sorry. I'm not sure I understand what you mean."

"Oh, I think you do," Mrs. Ralston said with her eyes narrowing and her arms folded across her breasts. "It would be extremely fortuitous if you were to marry Hunter and become the next Duchess of Willowbrook. Just think of all you would inherit."

Torie tried to hide her embarrassment and her anger. "That is far from my goal," she said. "I have never even met the Earl of Murdock."

"I'm sure you'll remedy that quite soon after he arrives, though, won't you?"

"I'm sure, Mrs. Ralston, that when he arrives I shall meet him, but I have no intention of doing anything more than showing him common courtesy. As I try to do with all people."

Torie gave Eulalia a sharp look, then stepped around her and descended the remaining steps. How daring of her to even think such a thing. Torie had never even met the duke's grandson. Although it was likely she would when he arrived for the holiday season, which was something she was looking forward to.

Torie wondered if Eulalia thought that was the only reason she came to sit with His Grace—because she wanted something from their friendship.

Her annoyance spiked. She didn't wish for anything from His

Grace. She had come the first few times as a favor to her grandmother, who considered him a dear friend, but then she realized that she truly enjoyed sitting with His Grace. She soon discovered how lonely the duke was, and saw how her visits cheered him up. Now she had become quite fond of him, and looked forward to her daily visits.

"Would you like a ride home, Miss Crawley?" Jenkins asked as he opened the door to allow her to leave.

"No, Jenkins. I think I need to walk home and clear my head."

"Pay her no mind," Jenkins said, lowering his voice and casting a glance back to the top of the stairs, where Eulalia had reached her room. "She's a wicked woman and she's jealous of anyone who isn't as miserable as she is."

"I think you understand her perfectly, Jenkins." Torie buttoned her coat and donned her gloves and neck wrap as she stepped out of the house.

"Good day, my lady. I look forward to seeing you tomorrow. You bring a ray of sunshine whenever you come."

Torie waved as she followed the path that took her home. She struggled to keep her mind from running away from her as she walked the narrow path that led from Willowbrook Manor. The first flakes of snow began to fall, and she pulled the collar of her coat higher around her neck and kept her head lowered.

How dare Eulalia hint that she sat with His Grace for the sole purpose of benefiting from his wealth? As if she needed the Duke of Willowbrook's money.

Torie trod lightly across the shallow dusting of snow that blanketed the ground as she passed the low boundary wall that separated Willowbrook Estate from Wickham Place. She would be glad when she reached home and could discuss what Mrs. Ralston had said to her. Her grandmama would know how to interpret what the woman had hinted at.

A large flake of snow landed on her cheek. Torie paused to whisk it away. When she lifted her gaze, she noticed smoke coming from the chimney of Mr. Jackson's cottage. That shouldn't be. Old man Jackson had gone to visit his son and daughter-in-law for the holidays. They had invited him for the Christmas season, and he'd left nearly a week ago.

Torie walked through the mounting snow, knowing she should check on the cottage for him. She looked through the window to see if someone had broken in.

The first strange thing she noticed was a fire blazing in the hearth. Next, she spied a cup and saucer on the table. She leaned to the side a bit in order to see further into the room and gasped. A man lay on the floor. He looked unconscious, and a puddle of blood appeared to have come from a wound in his shoulder.

Torie hurried around to the kitchen door, which opened freely when she pushed on it, and she entered. She stepped to where the man lay and felt his neck for a pulse. Nothing. Next, she felt his wrist. There was a faint pulse, and Torie breathed a sigh of relief.

She went to the kitchen cupboard and took a cloth from a drawer, then dipped the cloth into a half-filled bucket of water near the sink. When she returned to the injured man, she placed the cloth on his forehead, then opened his jacket, waistcoat, and shirt to check his wound. Before she could evaluate the extent of his injury, his hand reached up and his fingers clamped around her wrist.

"Don't move, sir," she said. "You're injured."

"Who are you?"

His voice was weak, and it took a great deal of effort for Torie to hear him.

"Victoria, sir. Victoria Crawley. I only mean to help. You've been injured."

He sank back in a helpless heap and closed his eyes.

"Can you sit?" she asked.

His head moved in a negative response.

"Well, you can't stay here. I need to get you home."

"Where's...home?"

"I live with my grandmother, the dowager Countess of

Wickham."

"She's your…grandmother?"

"Yes."

Torie rose and ran to the bedroom where she found several blankets. The man on the floor was shivering from the cold. After covering him, she drew several towels from a rack in the kitchen. She needed to stop his wound from bleeding. He'd already lost far too much blood.

"This is going to hurt, sir." She folded two small towels and pressed them against his wound.

He pressed his lips together against the pain, then groaned.

"I'm sorry, sir. But I have to stop the bleeding."

He didn't respond. Instead, he clutched the blankets she'd placed over him so tightly his knuckles turned white. A thick sheen of perspiration broke out on his forehead and huge drops of wetness ran down his cheeks.

Torie turned to the cupboards and rummaged through each one in search of a bottle of whiskey. She finally found one and took it back to the man and held it to his lips.

"Here, drink this."

She tipped the bottle to his lips, and he greedily drank. She placed the bottle in his hand and pressed on his wound again. He clutched the bottle and tipped it to his mouth himself.

"We can't stay here, sir. I need to care for you, and I don't have what I need to make you better."

He opened his eyes as if asking her what she intended.

"As soon as I get the bleeding slowed, I'm going to go home and return with a wagon and some men. Promise me you won't do anything foolish before we get back."

"Like…what?" he gasped.

"Like die," she answered.

She almost thought she saw a faint smile on his face, but knew that was impossible. He was in too much pain to muster a smile.

⫸⫷

WHEN TORIE MANAGED to get the bleeding slowed, she hurried from Jackson's cottage to Wickham Place as quickly as she was able in the snow. She rounded the stable and called for a wagon, then hurried to the house and collected everything else she might need to care for the wounded man. By the time the wagon appeared at the front door she had recruited three footmen and ushered them all into the wagon.

"Hurry! Get us to Mr. Jackson's cottage as fast as you dare!"

Once they arrived, Torie raced into the house, not knowing if she'd find the man she'd left a few minutes ago dead or alive, but when she knelt down beside him and reached for his hand, he squeezed her fingers. She'd never felt a relief so gratifying.

The men loaded him into the wagon, and Torie lifted his head to her lap as they returned to Wickham Place. When they reached her grandmother's house, the men carried him up the stairs and put him in one of the guest rooms.

The staff most able to care for him stayed with him, removed his clothes, and cleaned him up as much as possible.

"Did he tell you his name?" Torie's grandmother asked when she joined her on the landing outside his door.

Torie shook her head. "He was in too much pain to say much of anything."

"What does he look like?"

Torie looked at her grandmother and smiled. "He's big. I mean…big. It took all three of the men I took with me to lift him into the wagon. And I think he's good-looking. It was hard to tell." She turned her gaze to meet her grandmother's. "I think he was recently in the army."

"What makes you think that?"

"His boots. His clothes were common but his boots were like those that soldiers wear."

"Oh," the dowager Countess of Wickham said.

When the next upstairs maid came near, the dowager issued orders for her to have Cook bring a tea tray and a bottle of whiskey.

A short while later, Cook arrived. At the same time, the door opened and the men filed out.

"He's hurt bad, my lady," Pauly Burrows informed them. Pauly worked in the stables and was the closest thing to a doctor they had. "I got the bullet out, but we need to watch it real close so it don't get infected."

"Thank you, Pauly," the dowager said.

"Do you want me to stay for a while yet?"

"No. Get some rest, Pauly. We might have need for you yet tonight. I'll keep Stomes with me. We'll watch over him."

Stomes was Torie's personal maid, and there wasn't anything she could not do. Torie couldn't ask for a more proficient maid.

"Very well, my lady," Pauly said. "It's too bad Willowbrook doesn't have a doctor yet. One would really come in handy about now."

"I quite agree," the dowager said.

Pauly tipped his hat and left. When he was gone, a footman opened the door and stepped aside for the dowager countess and Torie to enter the room. Torie looked at the man on the bed. He was more pale than he'd been earlier, and if she were any judge, he had developed a fever.

She stepped to the bed and placed her hand on his forehead. He was warm but, thankfully, not burning up.

Torie turned her head and looked over her shoulder to where her grandmother stood, and her breath caught. Her grandmama's face had lost most of its color and her eyes were filled with tears.

"Grandmama?"

"By the saints," her grandmama whispered, then sank into the nearest chair.

CHAPTER TWO

"WHAT IS IT, Grandmama?" Torie ran to where her grandmother had sunk into the chair. "What's wrong? Are you all right?"

"Oh, Torie. Do you know who this man is?"

Torie looked at her grandmama in confusion. "No. Do you?"

"Yes. This is Hunter Melbourne, Earl of Murdock and heir to Willowbrook."

Torie stepped over to the bed and rinsed a cloth in the basin of cool water. She washed his face, then placed the cloth on his forehead. "This is His Grace's grandson?"

Lady Wickham nodded.

"We must send word to His Grace to tell him his grandson is here. He's been terribly concerned because Hunter hasn't arrived home yet."

"No. We mustn't tell him," Grandmama said.

Torie turned to face her grandmother. "Why ever not? He's very concerned for him."

"Look at him, Victoria."

"Are you afraid he might die?"

Her grandmother smiled as she shook her head. "No, he'll live. He comes from stock that's conditioned to survive. He won't die."

"Then what is it?"

"That's a bullet wound in his shoulder. Whoever shot him wants him dead."

A wave of fear stabbed inside Torie's breast. Who would want his lordship dead? It had to be someone who would benefit from his death. Someone like Frank Ralston or his son. Or perhaps an enemy he'd made during the war.

Torie rinsed her cloth in fresh, cool water and placed it on his forehead, then rinsed another cloth and placed it on his chest.

"I'm going to have Cook brew some tea with feverfew in it," her grandmother said. "Lace it with whiskey and have him drink as much of it as he'll take. I'll send up a tray for you, too. I imagine you haven't eaten since early this morning." The dowager turned to Torie's maid. "Be sure she eats it, Stomes."

Stomes curtsied.

"Thank you, Grandmama," Torie said as her grandmother left the room.

"Do you think someone really tried to kill his lordship?" Stomes asked as she straightened the bottles and bandages on the bedside table.

"We won't know until he wakes enough to tell us what happened," Torie said. "But it looks like someone may have."

"Who would do such a thing?" Stomes asked.

Torie shook her head. "I don't know, but they were quite serious in their attempt. And very nearly successful."

There was a knock on the door, and an upstairs maid entered with a tray for Torie and a cup of tea laced with feverfew for Lord Murdock. Torie added a bit of whiskey to his tea.

"Help me raise his head, Stomes. I need him to drink some of this."

Stomes stepped behind Torie and lifted Lord Murdock's head, then Torie held the cup to his lips and he drank a little. After the first sip, he turned his head and sputtered.

"You need this, my lord. It will help with the fever."

She held the cup to his lips again, and he took another sip. After he'd swallowed, he turned his head toward her and opened his eyes.

"Who…are…you?"

"I am Lady Victoria Crawley. The dowager Countess of Wickham is my grandmother."

His eyes shifted around the room. "Where…am I?"

"You are on my grandmother's estate, at Wickham Place."

He closed his eyes and breathed a deep sigh. "Have you sent…word to my…grandfather that I'm…here?"

"No," she answered.

"Good. Don't." He closed his eyes again.

"Here, my lord. Drink a little more before you go back to sleep."

She held the cup to his lips. Thankfully, he drank more before he fell asleep again.

While he slept, Torie rinsed another cloth in cool water and placed it on his forehead. "Would you get a fresh pot of hot water, Stomes? I want to make sure I have the feverfew-laced tea ready in case he wakes."

"Yes, miss," Stomes said, then left the room.

Torie placed her hand on his cheek and felt the warmth beneath her flesh. He was warm, but not overly hot. That was good. She placed her hand on the bed beside him. Unexpectedly, he reached out and clasped his fingers around hers.

He held them firmly, causing currents to race up her arm. She thought it was probably unwise to keep her hand connected to his, but couldn't bring herself to break their contact. There was a strength that passed from his fingers to hers. A connection that was unlike anything she'd experienced before.

"How is he?" her grandmother asked as she entered the room.

"He's no better," Torie answered. "But neither is he any worse."

"That is a positive sign."

"I sent Stomes down for another pot of feverfew tea."

Her grandmother sat in a cushioned chair near the bed and

focused on Lord Murdock. "He looks a great deal like his grandfather did at this age. More than his older brother, even."

"Did they both have such rich, dark hair?" Torie asked.

"His older brother's hair was much lighter. And his eyes were blue, the color of his mother's. Has he opened his eyes?"

"Yes. They are so dark they're almost black. Like his grandfather's," Torie answered.

"I always thought the duke's eyes were one of his most appealing attributes."

"You obviously cared for him, Grandmama. Why did you not pursue him?"

Her grandmother chuckled. "There wasn't an opportunity. Willowbrook was a second son, and his older brother was a magnificent example of strength and vibrant health. No one anticipated he would be felled by a fever. But a sickness spread through the area, and the elder Willowbrook was one of only three people who perished in the entire county."

"Oh my," Torie said.

"When the current Duke of Willowbrook came back to assume the title, he was already married and had one child, with a second on the way." Her grandmother cast a glance to the bed. "That would have been Stephen and Hunt's father. There was a third child—she was the oldest, a daughter. She died while still in her infancy.

"The duchess and I got along very well, and the duke and your grandfather became close friends. It was a sad day indeed when the duchess passed, and an even sadder day for me when your grandfather died. It took me a long time to recover from his death."

"What happened between my father and grandfather that put such distance between them?" Torie had often wondered. It must have been monumental, for not once in her entire life had her father spoken to his father. Nor had her father been to see his mother once in that same time. And every time she'd dared to bring up the subject of the Earl or Countess of Wickham, the subject was quickly brought to a halt.

"Has your father never said anything?" the dowager asked.

"No. He refuses to discuss the subject."

"Perhaps that's for the best, Victoria," her grandmother said on a sad sigh.

"Do you miss seeing Father?"

"Of course I do. He's my son."

"Have you ever encouraged him to visit you?"

"I shouldn't have to encourage him. He should want to come to see me."

"But if you—"

"Enough, Victoria. We've discussed your father's stubbornness long enough. Besides, he doesn't bear the entire blame. Some of it is mine."

Victoria had to agree with her grandmother. She'd only been allowed to stay with her grandmama instead of being exiled to Scotland because she threatened to run away and travel here on her own if her parents didn't allow it. And she was glad she'd come. Her grandmother was a fascinating woman, and Victoria would never regret one day of the time she'd spent living with her. They had a special bond, and she cherished it.

"I'm going to retire now," her grandmother said, rising from her chair and walking to the door. "Don't stay up too late. Are you going to spend time with His Grace tomorrow?" she asked before she left the room.

"Yes. I don't want to give anyone the impression that something is wrong. Or that I'm keeping something from them."

"That's wise. Just keep your ears open. Maybe you'll overhear something that's important."

Victoria nodded her agreement, then rushed across the room and wrapped her arms around her grandmother. "Good night, Grandmama. I love you," she whispered, then gave her grandmother a kiss on the cheek.

"Good night, sweetling," her grandmother answered, then left the room.

When Torie was alone, she returned to her chair beside the bed and sat. She poured fresh tea into a glass and added some of the feverfew Cook had mixed for his lordship. She waited until he stirred, then encouraged him to drink some.

"Who was…here?" he asked.

"My grandmama. She came to see how you are doing."

"Did you…tell her I was…still…alive?"

"No. I didn't have to. She said that you were much too stubborn to die on us—just like your grandfather."

His lordship tried to laugh, but he ended up moaning instead.

"Here," she said, holding the tea to his mouth. "Drink some more of your tea."

He did, and when he could take no more, Torie put the glass on the bedside table. She adjusted the covers and placed more cool cloths on his forehead. Then she sat down in the chair beside his bed.

"How long do you…intend…to stay here?" he said in a quiet voice.

"Probably most of the night. In case you need something."

"You don't…have to."

"I know, but I'm not tired, and I don't want to leave you alone."

She sat beside him a little longer without talking, in case he might fall back to sleep. But when he moaned in pain several times, she realized he probably wasn't able to sleep.

"Did you see who shot you?" she asked, trying to engage him in conversation.

"No. How did you…find me?"

"I saw the smoke coming from Mr. Jackson's chimney. He's visiting his son for the holidays, and I knew the cottage should be empty. I looked in the window and saw you on the floor."

"I managed to drag myself in here and kindle a fire before I passed out," Murdock said. "What were you doing…out there?"

"I was on my way home from visiting your grandfather. I go over nearly every day, mostly just to chat, or to read to him."

"Tell me about him. It's been...more than...three years since I've...seen him."

"He's quite concerned over you. He's anxious for you to return."

"I wish I could...tell him I'm...here, but...I can't until I...know who...tried to...kill me."

"Do you know why someone wants you dead?"

"For the...money."

"The money you will inherit when your grandfather dies?" Torie asked.

"That...and the trust...that was left...to my brother...from my father...which now passes down...to me."

"I take it that it's quite large," Torie said.

"Yes," Murdock answered.

Before either of them could say anything more, Stomes entered the room with a maid on her heels. She brought in a basin of fresh water, and the maid carried a tray with small sandwiches for Torie and a bowl of broth.

"Cook thought you might be hungry, and she sent up some broth for his lordship," Stomes said.

"Thank her for me when you return," Torie said to the kitchen maid.

The young girl bobbed a curtsy, then left the room.

"You need to go to bed, Stomes."

"What about you? I'll stay with his lordship, but I think you should go to bed."

Torie shook her head. "Pauly should be here shortly to check Lord Murdock's wound. When he arrives, I'll go to my room. I need to get a little sleep if I intend to sit with His Grace tomorrow. And you'll need to stay with our patient while I'm gone."

Stomes nodded her agreement, then left the room.

"I hate that I'm...putting you...out," Lord Murdock said.

"You're not. I'm relieved that I found you and brought you here."

"I am...too."

"Are you just home from the war?"

"Yes. I came with a friend. He'd been wounded…and they sent him home to…recover."

"Would I know him?"

"I doubt you'd know Ethan. Ethan Essex."

"It's a strong name," Torie said, trying to keep the conversation going.

"He's a…strong man. One of the…best shots in…the army."

"Does he live around here?"

"No," Lord Murdock answered. "He lives in…London."

"That's not far from here. We've had several of the nobility and newly rich commoners purchase land close by and move here. When Viscount Shelling died, his heir portioned his land and sold it in smaller parcels in order to pay his gaming debts. Those lots are being sold to the nobility and wealthy commoners, and Willowbrook is growing because people want to get out of London during the hot summer months and move to the country. I predict that, in time, Willowbrook will become quite a large city."

"That will be…exciting to see," he said.

"Yes, it will."

Torie watched her patient's eyelids flutter sleepily.

"Now, drink some of this tea and broth while they're hot." She poured some tea into a glass and held it for Murdock to drink, then fed him some broth. He didn't eat or drink much, but at least she got a little into him.

When he indicated he could take no more, she put everything back on the tray and straightened his covers. "Are you tired?" she asked.

"I think I'll…sleep…now," he answered, then closed his eyes.

Before she sat in her chair, she placed her hand on Lord Murdock's forehead. He was much warmer than he'd been earlier. In fact…

…he was burning up.

CHAPTER THREE

TORIE SPENT THE next several hours exchanging the warm cloths on his forehead with cool ones. He thrashed on the bed, tossing from side to side in an effort to escape the demons that haunted him. Whether they were demons that he'd brought home with him from the war, or the demons who had tried to kill him here, she wasn't sure. But from his violent thrashing, the threat he faced was very real to him.

"No!" he cried out, and threw his uninjured arm over his face as if to protect it.

"Lord Murdock," she said, trying to calm him. Her words had no effect on his tossing, and Torie chastised herself for referring to him as Lord Murdock. He hadn't been Lord Murdock long enough to recognize that she was speaking to him. "Hunter!" she called out even louder. "Major!"

He stopped thrashing for at least a few seconds, and Torie clasped her hands around his wrists. She knew she wasn't strong enough to stop him, but hopefully she could at least prevent him from doing himself any harm.

"Major! Wake up! Wake up."

"Are they here? Do you see them?"

Torie had no idea what he was talking about. She didn't know what world he was trapped in, but she knew she had to calm him.

"No, Major. They're gone. We're safe now."

He breathed a sigh of relief, then relaxed. "They're really gone?"

"Yes, sir. We're safe now."

"Has Tony come back yet?"

"Um…" Torie didn't know how to answer him. She didn't know who he was talking about. "No, Major. He hasn't returned."

"Find him!" he ordered her. "I have to find him."

Before Torie could protect herself, his lordship swung his arm through the air and knocked her off balance. She flew backward and landed on the floor. Before she could get to her feet, the door opened and Pauly ran into the room.

He raced to the bed and clamped his hands on his lordship's shoulders to hold him down. "Hand me the bottle of whiskey, my lady."

Torie grabbed the bottle from the bedside table and handed it to Pauly. He held it to his lordship's lips and let him drink. When he'd taken several healthy swallows, Murdock collapsed in exhaustion and lay without moving.

"I'm sorry, my lady," Pauly said. "I slept longer than I intended. I should have come sooner."

"That's all right, Pauly. He was asleep until a few minutes ago, then he woke and started thrashing on the bed. He's developed a fever." Torie rinsed a cloth in cold water and placed it on his lordship's forehead.

Pauly pulled back the bandage and checked Murdock's wound. "He's started bleeding again."

"Oh, no."

"It's not bad, so I should be able to get it stopped in no time."

Pauly worked on his lordship's wound while Torie continually put cold cloths on his forehead and body in order to bring down his temperature. It took longer than she expected before Pauly was done, but at last he stepped away from the bed and Torie was able to sit down in the chair. She was exhausted.

One of her hands rested on the bed while the other hung over the side of the chair. She sat up with a start when Lord Murdock's hand rested on top of hers.

"Did I hurt you?" he asked in a quiet voice.

"No. Are you all right?"

"Yes. I had a…nightmare."

"Do you get those often?"

"Often enough. I haven't had one…for a while, though. I thought maybe…they'd gone away."

Torie pulled her hand out from beneath his and rose from her chair. She was shocked by the loneliness she felt when their flesh was no longer connected. She rinsed another cloth and placed it on his forehead.

The earl turned his head, and his gaze locked with Pauly's.

"Lord Murdock, this is our man Pauly," Torie said. "He's the closest thing we have to a doctor here. He removed the bullet from your shoulder."

"I owe you, Pauly," his lordship said.

"My pleasure, your lordship. You'll want to keep that arm still for at least a week or two. Thrashing around like you did tonight didn't do it no good."

"I imagine not."

"I'm going down to the kitchen and get some more cloths," Pauly said. "I'll bring us up another bottle of whiskey. I imagine you could use a drink about now."

"Yes. I could."

"Then, when I return, *you* need to get some rest, my lady. You need some sleep if you plan on going over to see His Grace tomorrow."

Torie nodded. "You're right, Pauly."

Pauly left the room, and Torie straightened Lord Murdock's covers.

"Thank you, my lady," the earl said.

"It's Victoria," she said. "But everyone calls me Torie."

"I'm Hunt. Call me…Hunt."

"Very well, Hunt."

"Thank you…Torie."

"No need to thank me." Torie finished straightening the bed, then sat back in her chair. "Who is Tony?"

"Tony?"

"Yes, you called for him. You wanted to know if he had returned yet."

"What did you tell me?"

"That he hadn't. Who is he?"

"*Was* he."

"Oh. I'm sorry."

"It's the price of war. Not everyone who goes over comes back."

"Were you close?"

"Yes. Like brothers. There were three of us…that joined at the same…time. Tony, Ethan, and me. At least two of us came home."

"What was your rank?"

"Why?"

"I'm just curious."

"Major."

Torie smiled.

"What are you smiling for?"

"I'm smiling because you were quite agitated and I couldn't get you to calm. I took a chance and gave you an order. I said, 'Calm down, Major,' and you did."

"Smart thinking," he said.

"I was a bit proud of myself," Torie said with a smile.

Just then, Pauly re-entered the room. He poured whiskey into a glass and helped Murdock drink it.

Torie placed her hand on the earl's forehead. Still concerned, she took a clean cloth, rinsed it in the cool water, and placed it on his forehead. "You're not nearly as warm as you were before."

"I feel better," he replied.

"That's the whiskey talking," she teased him.

"Then I'd better drink some more."

Pauly filled his glass from the bottle and helped him drink.

"I think I'll go to bed now. Is there anything you need before I leave?" Torie asked.

"No."

She reached for the doorknob.

"My lady?"

Torie stopped and turned.

"Thank you. For everything."

A rush of heat enveloped her heart. The Earl of Murdock was more handsome than any man had a right to be, and his voice had a smooth, velvety tone that settled deep in her stomach and churned like a whirlpool in a stream.

She reprimanded herself for letting her emotions run away with her. Hadn't she learned her lesson before? Wasn't that the reason she'd left London and come to live with her grandmama?

"ARE YOU GOING to go to see the Duke of Willowbrook today?" Grandmama asked when Torie entered the breakfast room and sat at the table.

"Yes." Torie took a sip of the tea that a footman poured for her. "I was going to go later, but I stopped in to see our guest and he was sleeping, so I decided to go early and come home sooner."

"How is Lord Murdock?"

"He had a difficult night and the sleep he did get wasn't very restful, so hopefully he'll sleep late this morning. But he no longer has a fever, so that's a good thing." Torie began eating, then paused. "I met Eulalia Ralston yesterday."

Her grandmother smiled. "What did you think of her?"

"I think she is quite rude. She accused me of visiting His Grace because I wanted to sink my claws into the future Duke of Willowbrook."

"She said that?"

"Yes. She said that I only visited him because I was after the Willowbrook money."

Her grandmother laughed.

"I didn't think it was very humorous, Grandmama."

"I think it's hilarious," her grandmother said, wiping the tears that ran down her face. "She obviously doesn't know how much you are worth, Torie. If she did, she'd be throwing her son in your path."

"I haven't met him yet."

"Thank your lucky stars."

"Is he that bad?"

"With a mother like Eulalia and a father like Franklin, the poor boy doesn't stand a chance."

Torie finished her tea and slid back from the table. "Perhaps I'll have the opportunity to meet the men of the Ralston family today."

"We should have an interesting conversation tonight, then," her grandmother said. "What excuse are you going to use for leaving His Grace earlier than usual?"

Torie stopped and thought a moment. "I'll tell them that you had some correspondence you needed help with and I promised I'd be home early to help you."

"That should work," her grandmother said.

Torie gave her grandmother a kiss on the cheek. "I'll see you after lunch," she said, then went out to put on her coat, scarf, and gloves, and left.

The weather was a little warmer than yesterday, but the sky was overcast and cloudy. Torie thought it looked as if it could snow at any time, and she was glad she would be coming home early. She pulled her coat up around her neck and walked at a fast clip to Willowbrook Manor.

The door opened before she reached for the knocker.

"You are early this morning, my lady," Jenkins said as he took her coat and scarf.

"Yes, Jenkins. Grandmother has some correspondence she needs my help with, so I told her I'd come home early."

"That might be good, my lady."

Torie considered Jenkins' statement. "Is something wrong, Jenkins?"

"No, my lady. But we have guests."

"Guests?"

"Yes, they are friends of—"

"Who do we have here, Jenkins?" a handsome man with golden blond hair and striking blue eyes said. He strode up to Torie, took her hand in his, and brought it to his lips.

Torie wasn't accustomed to anyone paying her such rapt attention. He kissed her fingers, then held her hand in his far longer than was customarily allowed. Even when she tried to remove her fingers from his grasp, the man tightened his hold.

"You haven't introduced us, Jenkins. Who is this lovely lady?"

"Lady Victoria, allow me to present Mr. Stanley Fridgerton. Mr. Fridgerton, Lady Victoria Crawley."

"Lady Victoria," Stanley said with a perfectly executed bow. "What brings you to Willowbrook?"

"I have come to see His Grace. We are close friends and I came to inquire as to his health. And what brings you to Willowbrook, Mr. Fridgerton?"

"I am a close friend of Connor Ralston's, and have come to spend some time with him and his family."

"Were you invited, Mr. Fridgerton?"

"By Ralston?" he asked with a smirk on his face. "Not exactly."

"I thought not," Torie said in an accusing tone. "It would have been quite improper of Connor Ralston to invite you, since this is not his home and he has no right to make use of it as his own."

Fridgerton released a mocking laugh. "Oh my, Lady Victoria. You have a sharp tongue, and you definitely know how to use it."

"I didn't realize I'd said anything that wasn't true, Mr.

Fridgerton." He glared at her for several tense moments, then Victoria broke their contact. "How is His Grace, Jenkins?"

"He is anxious for your arrival, my lady."

"Thank you, Jenkins. I'll go in to see him immediately."

Victoria turned to escape the overbearing Mr. Fridgerton, but before she could leave him, he grabbed her hand and refused to let her go.

"I'm sure we'll meet again, my lady."

Victoria pulled her hand out of Fridgerton's grasp and spun away from him. On knees that threatened to buckle, she followed Jenkins up the stairs and out of Fridgerton's sight.

"Take care with that one," Jenkins said when they were at the duke's door. "I don't trust him. There's something evil about him."

"I couldn't agree more, Jenkins. Why do you think he's here?"

"I'm not sure, but I think the young Mr. Connor might owe the scoundrel a bit of money."

"And he's here to collect?"

Jenkins nodded.

"When did he arrive?"

"Last night. He came with a friend."

"What's the friend like?"

"No better than this one."

Torie breathed a shaky sigh, then went in to see His Grace when Jenkins opened the door.

The Duke of Willowbrook looked up when the door opened, and his eyebrows shot up in surprise. "Victoria! What brings you here so early?"

"I thought I'd come to see you this morning since I promised Grandmama that I'd help her with some correspondence this afternoon. Some days she has trouble writing."

"I know what she means. I have the same problem."

"If ever you need me to write for you, you have only to ask."

"I will," he said, then looked to the door as if checking to make sure it was closed. "Have you met our guests?" he whispered.

Victoria sat close to the bed so she wouldn't have to speak very loudly. "Yes. I met one of them. A Mr. Fridgerton."

"Isn't he a work of art?" the duke said.

Torie couldn't help but laugh at his choice of words.

"Having friends like that doesn't speak very highly of Connor, does it?"

"No, it doesn't," Torie answered. "Do you know why they are here?"

"No, but Jenkins tells me he overheard them speaking to Connor about some money he owes them."

"What are you going to do if Connor comes to you for the money to repay his loan?" Torie asked.

"It depends on how much he needs. I might tell him I have to think about it. Or I might give him the money if it will get Fridgerton out of here."

"Be careful, Your Grace. I don't like that man."

"Neither do I," His Grace said, then stopped talking when the door opened.

Thankfully, it was Jenkins. The butler entered quietly, then made sure the door closed securely behind him.

"Is everything all right?" Torie asked when Jenkins approached the bed.

"Yes. For now." He focused his gaze on her. "Did you say you needed to leave early today?"

"Yes, I told Grandmama I would be home in time for lunch."

"Then might I suggest that you wait up here until I come to escort you? I overheard Mr. Fridgerton's friend indicate he was anxious to meet you. I believe he is someone you may not wish to meet when you are alone."

"Thank you, Jenkins," Torie said. "I will stay another half-hour or so, then I will be ready to leave."

"Very good, my lady."

Torie and His Grace spoke an amiable half-hour, and right on time, Jenkins came to get her. He brought her cloak and scarf.

"I may not pay you a visit tomorrow, Your Grace," she said, donning her cloak and scarf. "I will have to find someone to accompany me when I come again."

"Thank you for braving it today," the duke said, squeezing her fingers.

She followed Jenkins down a back staircase and left Willowbrook through the kitchen door.

She hurried over a little-used path to reach Wickham Place without being seen, then stepped through the servants' door and breathed a deep sigh of relief. She had never been so glad to be home in her life.

She'd been able to avoid Fridgerton and his friend today, but knew that wouldn't work all the time. The day would come when she'd be forced to confront both fellows. She only hoped that when that day did come, she wouldn't be alone.

CHAPTER FOUR

TORIE ENTERED THE house and went to her grandmother's sitting area first. She wasn't there. Nor was she in the library or her study. When Torie failed to find her, she went in search of their butler. Wilkins would know where her grandmother was. He knew where everyone in the household was.

"Where is Lady Wickham, Wilkins?" she asked.

"I think she went to see your patient," the butler answered.

Torie climbed the stairs and entered Lord Murdock's room.

"Oh, good, Torie. You're back," her grandmother said when she entered.

"How is our patient?" Torie looked at Lord Murdock and thought he looked slightly improved over the previous evening.

"I think he's a bit better," her grandmother said.

"I am much improved," he answered with a crooked smile.

"Good. Have you had lunch yet?" Torie asked.

"Yes. I just finished. How did you find my grandfather?"

Torie didn't answer immediately.

"What is it? Is he ill?"

"No, he's not ill, but something is going on at Willowbrook."

"What?"

"Two guests have arrived, and from all indications they are not reputable people."

"What do you mean, they are not reputable people?" Murdock asked.

"Two men, a Mr. Stanley Fridgerton and his friend. I didn't meet the friend, but Jenkins is convinced he is not someone who can be trusted."

"What brought them to Willowbrook?"

"They came to see your cousin, Connor Ralston. It seems Mr. Ralston owes them some money, and from the threats they issued, it must be a great deal of money."

"Is Grandfather safe?"

"For the moment."

Hunt threw the covers back and swung his legs over the edge of the bed.

"What do you think you're doing?" Torie cried out, then ran to lift his legs back onto bed.

"I must…get to Willowbrook," he said, struggling to catch his breath.

"You need to do nothing of the sort. You are not strong enough yet. And if Fridgerton was the person who shot you, you'll be walking right into trouble."

Hunt sank back against the mattress. "I hate this," he said, his anger evident.

"Do you have anyone you can get in touch with who might be able to help you?"

He thought for a moment, then opened his eyes. "Yes, I do. Someone I served with in the war. Ethan Essex."

"I'll get you some paper and a pen and we'll write to him right now. You wouldn't need help if you were healthy, but you're not. You need someone who hasn't been shot to watch your back." Torie went to the desk and took out some paper. "Tell me what you want to say and I'll write it for you."

Hunt dictated, and Torie wrote down what he said. He told his friend that he'd been injured and needed help, that he was at Wickham Place, and asked if his friend could come as soon as possible.

When Torie finished the letter, she sealed it and took it to one of the servants so they could put it in the post. After she saw it safely off, she went back to Hunt's room to sit with him, but she found him asleep. Rather than wake him, she let him sleep and left his room.

"Is he resting?" Grandmama asked when Torie joined her in the dining room for lunch.

"Yes. I'll take him something to eat when he wakes. I think we should let him rest as much as he can. I don't think he's used to taking care of himself as he should."

"I think you are correct. He has a lot of his grandfather in him."

Torie smiled. "Yes. He does."

"Will His Grace be all right in a house with the men who arrived last night?" her grandmother asked, clearly worried.

"Jenkins will take good care of him, as will the rest of the staff. Hopefully, they will give up on the idea of getting any money from him."

"Do you think one of them might be responsible for the attack on Hunter?"

Torie nodded. "I think it's likely. And if it wasn't one of them, I would suggest we watch Connor Ralston. Or perhaps even his father."

"It's frightening to think what Ralston might have been involved in."

"Someone needs to straighten him out before it's too late," Victoria added.

Torie finished her lunch, then made a tray to take to Hunt. She climbed the stairs and entered Lord Murdock's room. He was still sleeping soundly, and she decided to let him sleep. She set the tray on the desk beneath the window and sat in the chair.

Her lack of sleep from the night before caught up with her, and before Torie knew it, she'd closed her eyes and was asleep herself.

She looked forward to a peaceful rest, but her conversation with Eulalia Ralston replayed in her mind. The woman's words were vindictive as she accused Torie of deceiving the Duke of Willowbrook. Victoria knew she hadn't, but what if His Grace thought her visits were for unscrupulous reasons?

Her eyes snapped open and she looked at the Earl of Murdock. What if he had died? Then Murdock wouldn't be next in line to carry the Willowbrook title. Frank Ralston would be.

Suddenly, she wanted to know what had happened to the Earl of Murdock's older brother—the brother that Hunt inherited his title from. She'd never heard. Surely he hadn't died in a mysterious accident. But what if he had?

Torie sat back in her cushioned chair and closed her eyes. Before she realized it, sleep was upon her.

HUNT WASN'T AWARE of the hour, but he knew it had to be later in the afternoon. The sun was starting to sink lower in the sky.

He glanced around the room and stopped when he focused on Victoria Crawley sleeping in the chair. The first thing he noticed was her golden hair tied back from her face. Several strands cascaded down and framed her heart-shaped face. Long brown lashes rested on her cheeks, giving her an angelic aspect.

As he watched, her lashes fluttered as she struggled to wake. From the look of it, she hadn't managed to get any more sleep than he had last night.

She took a deep breath, then fell back into peaceful slumber. He watched her. He knew it wouldn't be long before she woke, and he wanted to take the opportunity to study her. She was truly beautiful. He owed her a great deal for saving him and needed to thank her. He also wanted to get to know her better.

She was an intelligent woman, and he wanted to find out as much about her as he could. What he wanted to know first was what she was doing here when the Season was in full swing. She should be in London attending the numerous events hosted by the *ton*. Or attending the opera or the theatre. Instead, she was stuck in the country, far away from the nightlife in London.

She shifted her position, then ever so slowly opened her eyes.

"Hello," he said in greeting.

"Hello," she answered. "Did you get at least a little rest?"

"I did. Did you?"

"I did." She sat up in the chair, then stood. When she was on her feet, she walked over to him and placed her hand on his forehead. "You don't have a fever," she said before pouring some whiskey into a glass and mixing Cook's feverfew concoction into it. "Here," she said, handing it to him. "How do you feel?"

"Better," he answered, feeling grateful for another swallow of the whiskey. "Pauly did a good job digging the bullet out of my shoulder. It's healing already."

"Good."

He watched Torie step over to the dinner tray, admiring her grace as she moved.

"Here," she said, handing him a piece of bread topped with butter and a slice of ham. "Cook made apple pie and a rice pudding. There's coffee, too, but I'm afraid it's cold. I'll have the kitchen send a hot pot."

"No, don't bother. I'll drink it cold. It won't be the first time. You learn not to be particular in the army."

Torie moved everything, thoughtfully arranging it so things were within easy reach, then sat back in her chair.

"Have you heard anything more from Willowbrook?" he asked, then took a bite of his sandwich.

Torie shook her head. "How long do you think it will take your friend to get here?"

"I look for him to arrive the day after tomorrow."

"I'll be glad when he's here. I worry about His Grace and everyone else at Willowbrook."

"So do I." Lord Murdock stretched, then threw the covers off.

"What do you need?" Torie said, stepping over to the bed. He heard the worry in her voice.

"I'd like to walk a little. Would you help me?"

"Of course," she said, then held out the robe her grandmother had brought earlier for him. She helped him put it on, then stepped to his side and wrapped her arm around his waist. Hunter placed his arm across her shoulder and sensed the strength beneath her graceful poise. "We'll only go a little way," she said. "Tell me if you get tired."

He smiled on hearing her words and prayed for strength. God willing, he'd manage to stay upright and enjoy her lovely arm about his shoulders a good bit longer. And not embarrass himself by crumpling in a heap.

⇒⇒⇒⇐⇐⇐

TORIE OPENED THE door and walked with him out into the hall. They turned to the right and started walking. When they reached the end, Torie turned him so his back was to the window seat and helped him sit.

"How are you doing?" she asked.

"I'm doing fine. How is it possible that I can tire so quickly?"

Torie knelt in front of him and laughed. "You were shot," she teased him. "That has a tendency to steal your strength."

She locked her gaze with his, and a bolt of something electrifying traveled between them, connecting them.

"You are a special lady, Torie," he said in a soft whisper. "I owe you my life."

Torie couldn't stop a shy smile from forming. A magical spark ignited, and she felt the draw that brought them together. Then the Earl of Murdock reached out and cupped her cheek.

The pressure of his flesh on hers brought her closer to him until his mouth touched hers.

Victoria met his lips with a desperation she'd never experienced before. Oh, she'd been kissed before. More than once. But never had any kiss ignited need as this one did.

She wrapped her arms around Hunt's neck and leaned into him.

He deepened his kiss, and she answered his demands with a request of her own. He kissed her as if his kisses were an entreaty, a mandate that she was required to respond to.

His tongue skimmed along the seam of her lips, and she opened to him. She'd never experienced anything so erotic. Never experienced anything so all-consuming. Never experienced anything that caused her to evaluate what he was demanding of her.

And she knew that whatever he demanded, she was willing to give.

He kissed her again, then broke their kiss with an audible sigh. "I'm sorry. I should have asked permission before I kissed you," he said on a ragged sigh.

"Oh…no…" she objected, the only answer she was able to stutter in response.

The Earl of Murdock pressed his forehead to hers and laughed. She couldn't stop her own laughter from joining his.

"Are you all right?" she finally asked.

"I'm not sure," he answered. "I wasn't expecting that."

"Neither was I," Torie responded in a breathy voice. She struggled to get to her feet, feeling elated and at the same time embarrassed. "I should get you back to your room," she said, holding out her hands for him to take. "You need to get back to bed."

Hunt took her hands and rose. "If you say so." He groaned as she helped him stand. "Are you going to return to Willowbrook this afternoon?"

She shook her head. "I don't think I'll return there any more this week. I'm going to write to your grandfather and explain that I have the sniffles and don't want to risk giving them to him."

"You're afraid, aren't you?" he asked, lowering his gaze to look at her.

Torie was going to lie to him and say she wasn't afraid to go back, but that wouldn't be the truth. She *was* afraid. The men who had joined Connor Ralston had alarmed her.

"I shouldn't be," she admitted. "But I am."

"Then don't go near them alone. Wait until Ethan arrives. Make sure he's there to watch out for you."

They reached his room and Torie helped him inside, then led him to the bed.

"What if Fridgerton was the person who shot you?" Torie asked. "What would his reason be?"

"Money. If Fridgerton shot me, he intended to eliminate me. If I am eliminated, then Connor's father is next in line for the Willowbrook title, and the wealth that brings."

"Which is an astronomical amount," Torie finished for him.

"Yes," Hunt answered as he propped his head back on the pillow. His face had lost a great deal of its color, and Torie could see that he was in pain.

She poured some whiskey into a glass and added the feverfew tea to it. "Here, drink this."

His hands shook when he took it, then he put it to his lips. "Thank you," he said, then handed the empty glass back to her.

"You need to rest for a bit. I'm going to leave you alone for a while. Try to rest." Torie added a little more whiskey to the glass and put it on the bedside table within his reach. "I'll bring a dinner tray later. I imagine you're hungry."

"Perhaps Cook will have some leftover apple pie," he said with his eyes closed and a smile on his lips.

"Perhaps she might," Torie answered, and left his room with a chuckle.

She closed his door behind her and hugged her arms around her middle. She leaned against the wall and breathed a huge sigh. What had she just done? Her lips were still alive with the kiss she'd shared with the Earl of Murdock. Her nerves still tingled from being held in his arms.

What was she going to do about this?

CHAPTER FIVE

HUNT LAY IN bed unable to think of anything but the kiss he and Victoria had shared. He tried to fall asleep, but sleep was the furthest thing from his mind. He'd kissed her.

He hadn't had any intention of kissing her, but one look into her eyes, one glance at her kissable lips, and he'd lost all control. He couldn't stop himself from pressing his lips to hers.

What he wasn't prepared for, however, was the startling reaction of his body. The effect Victoria had on him was unnerving. No female he'd ever kissed had affected him like she did.

Hunt closed his eyes, but instead of it helping to dispel all thoughts of her, Victoria's face just appeared as vibrant and alive as if she were standing before him. He threw the covers off and sat on the edge of the bed. There was no use in summoning sleep when the competition for falling asleep was so monumental.

He rose and paced the room, then sat in his chair. Instead of thinking about Victoria, he would be better served by trying to figure out who had shot him.

He tried to list all the suspects. There was Connor, of course. The man was desperate for money, and if he eliminated Hunt, his father was next in line for the title. Then there was Connor's friend. Connor owed him a great deal of money, and the only way the friend would ever get repaid was if Hunt was eliminated, which would leave the door open for Connor's father to get the title. But, in both cases, the person next in line to die was Hunt's grandfather, the Duke of Willowbrook.

The blood in Hunt's veins turned to ice. He had to heal as quickly as possible. He had to get strong enough to keep his grandfather safe.

Hunt rose and dressed, then left his room and slowly descended the steps.

"What are you doing?" Victoria asked him from the bottom of the stairs.

"I'm coming down for dinner."

She chuckled, and a new warmth sprang up in his chest. He'd never heard such a sincere laugh.

"You don't want dinner," she teased. "You've been sitting in your room thinking about that apple pie Cook has left over from last night."

Hunt laughed, thankful that she didn't know that his thoughts had been about the kiss they'd shared earlier. "Well, do you think she might have some pie left?" he asked as he entered the blue room.

"I shall ask," Victoria said, leaving him alone in the room. "You are in luck, my lord," she said when she returned. "Cook happens to have a piece or two left."

"Oh," he sighed as he sat down. "That means I might be able to have a piece now, and another after dinner."

She clamped her hand over her mouth and laughed, a gleeful sound.

"Do I amuse you, my lady?"

"Did you eat this much when you were in the army?"

"No. I went hungry most of the time, which is why I need so much sustenance now. To make up for all the meals I missed."

The expression on her face turned more serious.

"It wasn't that bad, Victoria. We didn't starve."

"But you didn't have enough to eat, did you?"

"No. Food was always a commodity in short supply. Food

and warm clothes."

"Warm clothes?"

"It was freezing cold in the Crimea during the winter. There was no way we could stay warm enough. I thought I would never in my life be warm again."

He watched her eyes fill with tears.

"I've said too much. At least I stayed alive to come home. Many didn't."

"Yes, many didn't," she said with a catch in her voice.

Thankfully, at that moment a maid rolled in a tea cart, and true to Cook's word, there was a large piece of apple pie sitting in the center of it.

"Here," Victoria said, handing him the pie. "You can get started on your pie while I pour. How do you like your tea?"

"Simple."

"I should have known," she said, placing his tea with no milk or sugar on the table beside his chair.

He finished his pie in four or five bites, then reached for the tea. "I'm glad you don't plan to visit my grandfather tomorrow. When Ethan gets here, he can go along to protect you—should you need to be protected."

"The only thing I regret is that your grandfather doesn't know that you are safe. He's been anxious to have you home."

"I know, but that can't be helped. As soon as whoever shot me realizes I'm still alive, they'll try to kill me again."

"Have you any idea who it is? To my mind there are basically two prime candidates. Either your cousin Connor, or his friend."

"Or Connor's father, who will be the next to inherit the title before his son does."

"Oh, I didn't think about him," Victoria said.

Before either of them could say more, there was a commotion in the foyer, followed shortly by Wilkins' knock at the door.

"Yes, Wilkins?" Victoria said, and the butler entered.

"Lord Murdock has a visitor. A Mr. Essex."

"Show him in," Hunt said.

The butler stepped back, and Ethan Essex entered the room.

TORIE LOOKED AT Hunt's friend and smiled. He was nearly as tall as Hunt, which meant he was at least six feet in height. But Essex's hair was a dark shade of gold. His complexion was a deep bronze, which made Torie think he must have spent a great deal of time in the out-of-doors. But his eyes were his most prominent feature. They were a deep shade of blue, as deep as a cloudless sky in the summertime.

His cheekbones were high and sharply chiseled, and he had a cleft in his chin that deepened when he smiled—which he was doing as he walked into the room and crossed to where Hunt sat.

"Ethan," Hunt greeted his friend as he tried to get to his feet.

"Stay seated," Ethan said, holding out his hand to prevent him from rising. "You don't look like you're in any shape to be out of bed, let alone on your feet."

"I'm glad to see you, Ethan. I didn't expect you until tomorrow."

"I left the minute I got your letter. I knew if you were desperate enough to write me, it was important."

"Yes, it is."

"I can see that. I didn't think we'd have to worry about getting shot at once the war was over and we were on home soil."

"Neither did I, but I was wrong." Hunt turned his gaze to Victoria, who was on her feet and standing by her chair. "Ethan, allow me to introduce you to Lady Victoria Crawley. Torie, this is one of the best shots in the army, Lieutenant Ethan Essex. A man I am proud to call my friend. He saved my hide more than once in the Crimea."

HIS FRIEND STEPPED closer to Torie and took her hand. He bent and kissed the air above her fingers, then gave her one of the breathtaking smiles Ethan was known for. His smiles were guaranteed to cause females to swoon.

Hunt knew Torie wouldn't swoon, but a stab of jealousy raged inside him when she giggled, then returned Ethan's smile with one of her own.

"It's a pleasure to meet you, Mr. Essex. Please, have a seat. We were just having tea. Would you care for tea or something stronger?"

"Do you have brandy?"

"I do," Torie said as she moved to a side table and poured some brandy into a glass. She delivered it to her guest and returned to her seat.

"I'm glad you're here," Hunt said. "I need to heal a little more before I'm able to look out for myself and my grandfather."

"Are you thinking someone will try to do him harm, too?" Ethan asked.

"Yes."

"If you gentlemen will excuse me," Torie said, "I must tell Cook we'll have a guest for dinner." She looked at Hunt and smiled. "And I'll be sure to tell her to save that extra piece of pie for our guest, since you've already had a piece today."

"Oh, that's cruel, Torie," Hunt mocked. "Cruel."

Her smile broadened, then she turned and left the room.

Hunt saw the smile on Ethan's face as Torie left and sat up straighter. "She's off limits, friend."

"I was afraid of that. She's far too gorgeous for you to pass by."

"And far too companionable."

Ethan rose. "Would you like something stronger than that cup of tea?"

"Yes. I definitely need something stronger. See if there's some whiskey over there."

Hunt's friend went to the liquor table, lifted a crystal decanter, and sniffed it. Acknowledging the whiskey with a grateful smile, he poured a generous amount into a glass. He gave it to Hunt and sat down.

"Give me the entire story, Hunt. Who wants you dead?"

"I'm not sure."

"Are you telling me there's more than one possibility?" Ethan asked with raised eyebrows.

"At least three that I know of."

"Hell, when you get into trouble, you get into *big* trouble."

"I know. And I haven't even been home yet."

"Very well. Start at the beginning. Tell me what's going on."

Hunt told Ethan the details of what had happened from the time he arrived home until Torie found him in the cottage and saved him. He explained who he thought might be behind the attempt on his life and why, and shared the reason each one of the suspects might want him dead. And that reason was money.

Hunt had just completed his tale when Victoria came back into the room.

"All I can say," Ethan said to Victoria, "is that the major here knows how to make enemies without even trying."

"Yes, he certainly does," Victoria said with a concerned expression.

"So, what's the plan?" Ethan asked before taking a sip from his glass.

"I need you to go to Willowbrook and keep an eye on my grandfather," Hunt said. "When Lady Victoria goes over to visit my grandfather, as she does nearly every day, keep an eye on her, too."

Ethan turned his attention to Victoria. "Who are you most concerned with?"

"For myself, the man called Fridgerton," she replied. "He's frightening. He has a nasty disposition. He came with another man who I have not met as yet."

"Who do you think poses the greatest threat to the Duke of Willowbrook?" he asked Victoria.

Torie shifted her gaze from Hunt to Ethan.

"Who, Torie?" Hunt asked.

"Your cousin, Hunt. Connor."

He couldn't hide his surprise. "Connor? You think Connor might want to harm my grandfather?"

Victoria nodded. "Jenkins has made the duke's bedroom off limits to everyone but family. Which means that Fridgerton and his friend cannot get near His Grace. But Connor can still get in. So, if he intends to do your grandfather harm, he's the only one who has easy opportunity."

"Your friend has a good head on her shoulders, Hunt," Ethan said.

"Yes," Hunt agreed, smiling at her. "She does." He reached for Torie's hand. "Are you going to see His Grace tomorrow?"

"I wasn't going to, but I've changed my mind. I think someone needs to be with His Grace around the clock."

"That's probably wise," Ethan said.

"I can sit with him during the day," Torie explained, "but not as much in the evening or during the night. That, I'm afraid, will be the most dangerous time for him."

"I think you're right," Hunt said.

"I'll make sure Jenkins assigns two footmen to stay with His Grace from the time I leave until I return," Torie said.

"That's a perfect plan, my lady," Ethan said. "I'm glad you returned to join us."

"Actually, I came to announce that dinner is ready. Grandmother is already in the dining room."

"Good," Hunt said. "I'm starving."

"You are always starving," Ethan said, then stepped over to help Hunt from his chair. When he was upright, Victoria took his arm to help him into the dining room.

There, Hunt introduced Ethan to the dowager countess before they sat down to eat.

"How did Hunt's brother die, Grandmama? Do you remember?"

"Why are you interested, Victoria?" the dowager countess asked. "That was a very sad time for His Grace."

"I'm sure it was," Torie replied.

Hunt stopped eating for a second and paid closer attention to Torie's question. "But why are you asking, Victoria?"

She looked at him, and he could see that she had a thought that was bothering her. But Hunt had been thinking the same thing. What if Stephen's death hadn't been an accident?

"I just wondered," Torie said. "I've never heard."

"Do you think there's a connection between my brother's death and the attempt on my life?"

"It's probably silly, but I just had a thought and couldn't get it out of my mind."

"How did my brother die, my lady?" Hunt asked the dowager countess. Suddenly the idea that the two events might be connected seemed more probable, and if they were, Hunt wasn't going to let the man responsible for Stephen's death get away with it.

Someone was going to die.

"Your brother died in a riding accident. He was known to race his horse every morning through Hyde Park. He'd always been an excellent horseman, and it wasn't unusual for him to ride much too fast. One morning, the cinch on his saddle broke, and he was thrown from his horse. He broke his neck in the fall."

"Did Grandfather think there was anything suspicious about it?"

"Actually, yes, he did. One of the stable hands said it looked like his cinch had been cut. Your grandfather voiced his concern, but everyone dismissed him because he was so overwrought. He took your brother's death quite hard."

Hunt was quiet for several moments.

"What are you thinking, Hunt?" Ethan asked.

"I wonder if the stable foreman still has Stephen's saddle."

"When I'm there, I'll visit the stable and do some looking around," Ethan said.

"Yes. Then let me know."

"I will."

After dinner, they retired to the burgundy room, which was Torie's favorite receiving room, and planned how they were going to execute their plan to draw out the person who had tried to kill Hunt. Then they hatched a plan to make sure they kept the Duke of Willowbrook safe.

Hunt would give anything to be able to visit the stable himself, but he couldn't yet. He wasn't strong enough to take part in their plan, and he would only be a hindrance and possibly get Ethan killed. So, regretfully, he promised to spend the next few days getting plenty of rest so he could be of some use when Ethan and Torie needed him.

Later, they all retired for the night. Torie and Hunt showed Ethan to a room, then they walked down the hall to Hunt's room.

"This is becoming more serious, Victoria. I can't bring myself to let you sit unprotected with my grandfather."

"What are you going to do? Come with me and hide in an armoire and jump out if someone tries to harm me?"

Hunt smiled, then placed his fingers on the nape of her neck and held her close. "No, I'm going to send one of your grandmother's footmen with you to protect you. Which footman would you like to accompany you?"

Victoria tilted her face and locked her gaze with his. "You are serious, aren't you?"

"Deadly."

"That's not necessary, Hunt."

"I say it is," he said. "So, which footman do you want to go with you?"

The expression on her face sent a wave of warmth rushing through his body. "Davey will do," she answered.

"Davey it is," he said, then lowered his head and kissed her. He didn't intend to let himself get carried away, but before he knew it, he couldn't get enough of her lips pressed to his and her body in his arms. He deepened his kisses and reveled in the feelings they launched.

When neither of them could breathe, he lifted his mouth from hers and gathered her closer. "Do you know how special you are?"

"Why?" she asked. "Just because I saved your life?"

Hunt's breath caught, and he burst out laughing. "Yes, that. And your sense of humor," he said, laughing until he hurt so badly he couldn't laugh any more. "Where do you come up with such humorous comments?"

"I keep them locked away inside me, and only let them come out when you least expect them. I like to surprise you."

"You're definitely good at that," he said, giving her a gentle squeeze. "Now go to bed before I can't bear to let you out of my arms."

"It's a good thing you are injured, or I might consider that," she said with an ample bit of sass, then turned and left him.

Hunt watched her walk away and knew without a doubt that he loved her. He didn't know when it had happened, or how. He'd always hoped he'd meet the love of his life someday, but he never thought it would happen. Not here. Not now.

He wasn't sure he even believed in love. That was an emotion he'd never experienced before, and he wasn't sure it even existed. And then he'd met Victoria and been forced to change his mind. Now he knew without a doubt that love existed, that it was real, because he couldn't imagine a life without her.

CHAPTER SIX

Victoria rose early in the morning and went down to breakfast. She wanted to speak with Ethan before he left, but he was already gone by the time she walked into the breakfast room. Hunt was there, however.

"Is Ethan gone?" she asked. Hunt started to get to his feet, but Torie stopped him. "Please, stay seated," she said. "No need to stand on formalities. You don't need to stand when I enter a room, and I can fill my own plate."

Hunt sat back in his chair and watched her. "How did you sleep?" he asked when she placed her plate on the table and sat next to him.

"I slept all right except for thinking about what was going to happen today."

"Don't worry, Torie. Ethan will watch over you. He'll make sure you're safe, and I intend to speak with Davey before you leave and make sure he knows exactly what is expected of him."

Victoria took a sip of her tea then set her cup back in its saucer. Her hands shook ever so slightly. Hunt noticed and placed his hand over hers and squeezed her fingers.

"I wish I could go with you." The serious look on his face told her how much he was worried over her.

"You just spend the day taking care of yourself so you heal faster. You'll have plenty of time to insert yourself in the middle of this mess when you're healthier."

Hunt smiled at her, and her heart swelled in her breast.

"What excuse is Ethan going to give your grandfather for being there?" she asked.

"He's going to tell him that we served in the army together and that I invited him for the holidays. He'll tell him that he had nowhere else to go, so he took me up on my offer and decided to arrive a few days ahead of me."

"That should ease your grandfather's mind. Maybe he won't worry about you so much."

"I can only hope," Hunt said.

Victoria and Hunt carried on a conversation until she finished her breakfast, then she rose from the table. "I'm going to tell Grandmama that I'm going to leave and inform her that I'm taking Davey with me."

"Do you think that's wise?"

"I think it's better to tell her everything so she knows what's going on than have her realize Davey's missing and think the worst."

"I suppose you're right," he said, then released her hand. "I'm going to give Davey a few last-minute instructions," he said. "Then I'll wait here for you until you're ready to leave."

Victoria nodded her agreement, then ascended the stairs to say goodbye to her grandmama. Today promised to be a very interesting day.

VICTORIA SAT IN the carriage as it travelled the short distance to Willowbrook Estate. Part of the plan was for Davey to deliver her to Willowbrook, then take the carriage to the stable. When she was ready to leave, he would drive her back home. She was glad Davey would be with her, and that she wouldn't be on her own where Bridgerton could waylay her.

She felt quite safe with Davey. He was nearly as tall as Hunt, and as broad in the shoulders. She guessed Davey was as strong, too. He was quite comparable to Hunt, as was Ethan.

When they arrived at Willowbrook, Davey deposited her at the front door, and Jenkins stood to greet her.

"Oh, my lady. His Grace will be awfully pleased to see you've come today."

"Is everything all right, Jenkins?" she asked.

"Yes, everything is well. He simply missed you yesterday. It was a long day for His Grace."

Torie smiled. "Well, I'm here today." She turned to face Davey. "Jenkins, this is Davey. He will be spending the day with me today."

"Yes, my lady. That's a wonderful idea. If not, I was going to suggest that I assign one of His Grace's footmen to stay close to you."

Jenkins accompanied Torie inside and took her cloak and scarf while Davey took the carriage to the stable.

"We have another guest, my lady."

Torie looked at Jenkins.

"This is a friend of Lord Murdock's. He claims Lord Murdock invited him to spend the holidays with him. I didn't know what to do, so I showed him to a room. I explained that Lord Murdock hadn't arrived yet, but he said that was all right, he'd wait for him."

Victoria thought for a moment, then decided that Jenkins needed to know everything that was going on. She stopped at the bottom of the stairs and walked into one of the rooms at the end of the hall. Jenkins followed.

"Is something wrong, my lady?" he whispered.

"Yes and no, Jenkins. Lord Murdock is at Wickham Place."

"He is home?"

"Yes, but he was injured. Someone tried to kill him."

Jenkins reacted exactly as Victoria expected him to. His hands clenched into fists and his eyes narrowed as if he wanted to hit someone.

"Did he see who the villain was?"

Torie shook her head.

"I can make a guess and come up with three possibilities," Jenkins said.

"I can, too," Torie answered.

"Will Lord Murdock be all right?"

"Yes. He wrote to Mr. Essex to come to Willowbrook and watch over his grandfather until he was well enough to watch over him himself."

"I feel much better now, my lady. I've been worried about His Grace. He's been quite unsettled. He's concerned about Lord Murdock."

"I'll try to reassure him, Jenkins."

"Very well, my lady."

Victoria turned to leave the room, then stopped. "Oh, one more thing, Jenkins. Would you make sure you are with Cook when she dishes up His Grace's meal, then bring his trays up to him yourself?"

"Do you think—"

"No, no. I'm just being overly cautious."

"Very well, my lady."

"Very good. Now, let's go see His Grace. And show Davey up when he comes in, would you?"

"Yes, my lady."

Victoria left the room and took the stairs to His Grace's room. The look of happiness on the Duke of Willowbrook's face when she walked through the door was worth the world to her. She couldn't wait until Hunt was well enough to see his grandfather. That would be another special moment she didn't want to miss.

SEVERAL DAYS PASSED in calm nonviolence. At least, there was nothing that drew Victoria's attention other than Fridgerton's daily effort to find her alone and attempt to trap her in an unoccupied room or a hallway closet. Thankfully, Davey was right behind her and prevented Fridgerton from getting to her.

Meal times were the most stressful. The Duke of Willowbrook had improved to the point where he was able to leave his room and join his guests for lunch. Victoria accompanied His Grace to the dining room, where he sat at the head of the table. Franklin Ralston always sat at the opposite end, already signaling that he was next in line for the Willowbrook title, should Hunt not live to assume it. Although Ralston never said that aloud.

Connor sat to his father's right, and Eulalia sat to her husband's left. The more Victoria came to know the Ralstons, the less she liked them. Franklin wouldn't have been so bad if his wife didn't constantly encourage him to assume his *rightful* place in the household, and if she allowed him to be the head of his own family, instead of telling him every move to make.

Victoria didn't know what to say about Connor, other than he'd been coddled and spoiled, and was used to getting whatever he wanted. He was younger than Hunt's eight and twenty, but not by more than three or four years. If he had a brain in the head that sat on his shoulders, it had atrophied long ago from lack of use. There was no need for him to use his brain when his mother did all his thinking for him.

Victoria was sure Connor Ralston's daily existence consisted of gambling, drinking, and womanizing. No wonder he was involved with a man such as Fridgerton. No doubt he owed money to many more lenders than just this one. But if Torie were Connor, she'd be frightened to death that whatever His Grace gave him at Christmas wouldn't be enough to pay his debts, and she wasn't sure what Fridgerton would do to get the money he was owed.

"Lady Victoria," Fridgerton said, speaking loud enough that everyone at the table could hear. "How is it that you have escaped having a husband and several children by your advanced age?"

His Grace placed his fork on his plate with a loud thud, then stared at Fridgerton with an icy glare.

Ethan gripped his knife in his fist as if he was prepared to stab Fridgerton with it.

Eulalia snickered loudly behind her linen napkin, and Connor took a swallow of his wine and made a choking spectacle of himself.

Fridgerton's friend slapped Fridgerton on the back and congratulated him.

"Well, Lady Victoria?" Fridgerton said.

Torie gently put her fork on her plate and dabbed at her mouth. "I'm just lucky, I guess. Most of the men I've met are as rude and lacking in manners as you, Mr. Fridgerton. The women of my acquaintance are blessed with a certain amount of common sense and would rather be dead than spend any amount of time in such an unpleasant man's company. Is that perhaps why you are not married at your advanced age either, Mr. Fridgerton? Do most women choose to avoid you because of your lack of manners?"

Fridgerton's eyes thinned to narrow slits that glared at her with icy anger. "You have a sharp tongue you should learn to control, my lady. The day may come when someone teaches you a lesson in that regard."

"Well, that someone will not be you, Mr. Fridgerton."

"Perhaps not," Fridgerton countered. "But there's nothing I would enjoy more than teaching you to control your outspokenness."

"Enough, Mr. Fridgerton!" the duke yelled, slamming his fist down on the table. "You have insulted my friend for the last time. Please pack your belongings and leave my house."

"But Your Grace—"

"Now!"

"You'll regret this, Your Grace," Fridgerton threatened.

"I already regret allowing you to take advantage of my hospitality only to insult my guests," the duke said in an angry voice.

Fridgerton slid his chair back with a harsh movement, and his friend and Connor joined him and left the room.

No one spoke after they left.

Victoria felt a wave of guilt after the room was cleared of the three men. She folded her napkin and rose from her chair. "Please, excuse my rudeness, Your Grace. My outburst was—"

"Totally understandable, Victoria. Fridgerton was at fault for what happened. No one speaks to a lady as he did you without having to answer for his rudeness."

"Thank you for understanding," she said. "Please, excuse me."

Victoria left the room and walked to the solitude of the library. She needed to be alone. She needed to consider the rudeness of her words. It was totally uncalled for. She'd allowed herself to stoop to the level of Fridgerton's rudeness.

That was the reason she was here, the reason she'd come to stay with her grandmother. Her father had given her the choice between coming to spend a year with her grandmother in hopes that she would learn self-control, or going to the Earl of Wickham's northernmost estate in Scotland until she'd learned some decorum. Only then would she be allowed to return home.

Victoria had never been to her father's estate in Scotland, but her mother had. If her description had been accurate, there wasn't a more deserted and isolated area in all the world. Victoria knew if she was sent there, she'd never survive. She chose to go to her grandmother's. At least with her Grandmama, she stood a decent chance of learning to control her temper. Except today had proven she had no more control over her wayward tongue or actions than she'd had in London.

Victoria rose to her feet and paced the room from one end to the other. When she passed the window that overlooked the garden, which in the spring and summer would be filled with a variety of flowers blooming in every imaginable color, she stopped. The door to the library opened while she was standing at the window.

She didn't turn around to see who it was. She was sure it was His Grace, or perhaps Mrs. Ralston coming to reprimand her for causing her son's friends to be asked to leave.

"I have come in here to be alone," she said softly.

"Have you, my lady?" an angry voice said from behind her.

Victoria turned around and faced a livid Fridgerton. She tried to plot the nearest escape route to get away from him, but she was trapped.

He took a step toward her.

"Get out!" she demanded.

His lips thinned as he snarled at her. "You think you can order me around, Lady Victoria? Well, you can't."

He took another step toward her, and when he reached her, he clasped his fingers around her upper arms. He was hurting her, but she refused to cry out. She wouldn't let him see her pain.

"Let me go!" Torie growled. She tried to twist out of his grasp, but his hold on her only tightened.

"Do you have any idea what you cost me?" he asked, moving his hands to her wrists. With a quick jerk, he pulled her hands behind her back and caught both her wrists in his massive grasp.

"Let me go, you oaf," she said.

He laughed, then pressed his lips to her throat. He kissed her face and her throat and her forehead, then lowered his mouth to her lips.

Victoria was afraid she might vomit on him, and thrust her knee into his groin. "Let me go!" she screamed.

"Bitch!" he snarled, and slapped her.

She managed to get one hand free of his grasp and scraped her fingernails down his cheek.

"Bloody hell!" he bellowed, then slapped her harder than before. He threw her against the wall, then lifted his hand back to slap her again.

Torie closed her eyes to keep from seeing his hand coming at her. Her head bounced against the wall and her world turned black. She refused to lose consciousness for fear of what he'd do if she wasn't able to fight him.

He hit her again, then suddenly, Fridgerton's weight was lifted off her. She struggled to focus on what was happening, but her vision blurred and she couldn't make out the figures in the room.

As her vision slowly cleared, she realized that Ethan and Davey had come to her rescue.

"You're a dead man, Fridgerton," Ethan growled, then hit Fridgerton again. Ethan pulled him to his feet, dragged him across the room, and threw him out the door.

"Ethan?" Torie whimpered.

"Yes, my lady. Stay still. Don't try to get up. Get the wagon and bring it to the front, Davey."

"Davey?" she asked.

"Yes, my lady. I'm going to get the wagon. I'll take you home."

"Yes, I'd like to go home," she said, hearing her words oddly slurred.

Victoria felt more than heard Davey rush from the room as she closed her eyes again.

"Are you hurt?" Ethan asked.

"No. I'm fine."

"You're not fine," he said, turning her head and holding her hands. "But I don't think you're badly hurt."

"No, I'm not badly hurt. And what happened was my fault. My father told me my tongue would get me into trouble if I didn't learn to curb it."

"What happened wasn't your fault, my lady. You stood up to Fridgerton. Hunt would be proud of you."

"Oh," Torie said, opening her eyes. "Promise you won't tell him, Ethan. I don't want him to know."

"Why not? He'd be proud of you."

"No! Promise you won't tell him."

"I won't have to, my lady. All he'll have to do is look at you and he'll know. Your eye and cheek are already turning dark where Fridgerton hit you."

Torie brought her hand to her face, then moaned and pulled it away when a stabbing pain hit her. "What am I going to do?"

"You're going to tell Hunt exactly what happened here today. Then you're going to rest in bed for at least a day or two."

"I can't," Victoria argued. "His Grace needs me to sit with him."

"Perhaps your grandmother can call on him tomorrow."

The door opened and Davey entered. "The carriage is ready," he said.

Ethan helped Torie to her feet, then took the cloak Davey handed him and wrapped it around her shoulders. He led her down the stairs and caught Jenkins' eye when they reached the foyer.

"Oh, my lady. What happened to you?" the butler asked.

"I fell, Jenkins," she lied.

"No, Jenkins. The lady didn't fall. Mr. Fridgerton struck her."

"But don't tell His Grace," Victoria pleaded. "Just tell him I was embarrassed after my outburst during lunch and chose to go home."

"Yes, my lady. Are you sure you are all right?"

"I'm fine, Jenkins. I just want to go home."

"Of course, my lady."

The butler opened the door, and Ethan escorted her to the waiting carriage. Davey was already seated on top, and as soon as the door swung shut, the carriage rolled down the lane.

Victoria leaned back against the cushion, then looked out the window. When she focused on the interior, her eyes locked on Ethan. He sat opposite her and watched out the window, a gun in his hand. He looked ready and able to fire it at any moment.

"Do you think you're going to need that?" she asked.

"I can only hope. There's nothing I'd like more than to put a bullet through Fridgerton's black heart."

Ice water raced through Victoria's veins. If this was how Hunt's friend felt about what Fridgerton had done, she didn't want to even consider how Hunt would take the news.

CHAPTER SEVEN

FOR A FEW seconds, Victoria thought she might manage to sneak up to her room undetected. But she only reached the second step before Hunt stopped her.

"Victoria?"

Torie stopped, but didn't turn around. Although she wasn't brave enough to look in a mirror, she could imagine what her face looked like. It was unbearably sore to the touch and her flesh felt as if it was on fire. She knew it must have begun to discolor.

"What's wrong?" Hunt's voice brimmed with concern, and she heard his boots slam on the foyer tiles as he came toward her. "Turn around."

When she didn't immediately turn, he placed his hands on her shoulders and turned her so she faced him.

"Bloody hell!" he bellowed. "Who did this to you?"

"I—" She started to tell the lie she'd been practicing in her mind all the way here, but her gaze locked on where Ethan stood close behind Hunt. He shook his head to warn her not to even try to lie to Hunt.

"What happened?" Hunt took her hands and helped her down the steps until she stood on the bottom step and they were eye to eye with each other.

Victoria opened her mouth to tell Hunt what had happened, but before she could say the first word, her throat constricted and tears spilled from her eyes.

"Who did this?" Hunt asked, turning to face his friend.

"Fridgerton," Ethan replied. "Lady Victoria stood up to him when he insulted her, and he took exception to what she told him. The duke was angry with Fridgerton's behavior and demanded that he leave his house. Then Fridgerton waited until Lady Victoria was alone and attacked her. I didn't get to her in time to stop him."

"He's a dead man," Hunt growled. "Did he do anything else to you, Torie?"

"No, Hunt," she replied. "He tried to kiss me, but I stopped him. I kicked him where my brothers taught me it would hurt a man most."

"Good for you," Hunt said with a smile on his face, then he wrapped his arms around her and held her close. "Come with me. We need to get some cold cloths on those bruises."

Hunt took her to a receiving room and had Wilkins bring a basin of cold water and some cloths. "If you have comfrey or yarrow, bring that, too, Wilkins."

While they waited for the water, Hunt poured her a glass of wine. He also poured himself and Ethan glasses of brandy. When Wilkins came with the water, Hunt asked him to tell the dowager countess that Victoria had been injured and for her to join them. The butler left right away, and it wasn't long at all before the dowager countess joined them.

"What happened?" she asked, as she hurried to Victoria's side.

Ethan related the story while the dowager countess pressed cold cloths on Torie's face.

"I'm sure it looks worse than it is," Victoria told her grandmother.

"Perhaps, but I doubt it. Is this Fridgerton fellow still at Willowbrook?"

Victoria shook her head. "His Grace ordered him to leave."

"Good. Where do you think he went?"

"I don't know," Victoria answered. "Probably the Willowbrook Ale House. Connor Ralston went with him and his friend."

"Good. That's exactly where they belong."

"Grandmama, would you consider going to sit with His Grace for a few days? I don't want him to be alone, and I can't let him see my face. He'll feel worse than he already does."

"Of course," her grandmother answered. "Under one condition."

"What's that?"

Her grandmama turned to look at Hunt. "Tomorrow you will go to see your grandfather so he knows you're alive. Now that Fridgerton and Connor Ralston are out of the house, he deserves to know what happened to you and that you're well."

"Yes," Hunt answered. "That's only right. It will be his early Christmas present."

"Call it what you want, but he needs to see you. It will mean the world to him."

"Yes, it will," Victoria agreed. "I wish I could be there to see his face."

"But, of course, you will remain here and take care of yourself," he said.

"Yes, she will," Ethan said. "And I will stay here with her."

Hunt nodded in agreement. "You need to rest now," he said, then settled her on the sofa and placed a cover over her. "Does your head hurt? And don't lie to me," he warned her.

Victoria smiled. "A little."

"I'll get you more wine."

He took her glass and poured a little wine into it.

"What do you think Fridgerton and Connor are going to do?" she asked.

"Connor needs the money His Grace gives him each Christmas too badly to leave before Christmas morning, so he'll stick around. Fridgerton won't dare show his face, so he'll either stay out of sight, or return to London."

"I hope he goes back to London. I prefer to never see him again."

"That would be my choice, too," Hunt said. "But I doubt he's that intelligent. He'll probably stay around so when Connor gets his Christmas money, he's there to receive his portion."

Just then, the dowager countess came back into the room with her heavy cloak, gloves, and hat on. She was ready to travel to the Duke of Willowbrook's mansion.

"Are you ready?" she asked, and Hunt rose.

"Did you tell Wilkins to tell Davey to go with you?"

"Yes. He's waiting by the carriage."

"Good." Hunt turned to Ethan. "Be sure she doesn't get up."

"Yes, Major," he answered.

Hunt reached down and took Torie's hand in his. He gently squeezed her fingers, then left the room with her grandmother.

As soon as they were gone, Ethan took the glass from her hand and set it on the table. "Now, sleep for a while," he said, then walked to a wall with shelves of books and chose one. He sat with it in his lap and opened it, then started reading.

"You didn't strike me as a man who enjoyed reading," she said, watching him turn the pages.

"My father owns a bookshop in London. I spent my youth surrounded by books, by reading."

"How wonderful," she said.

"Yes, it was. I read everything I could put my hands on."

"That must have been a wonderful childhood," Torie said, then closed her eyes and, thanks to the wine she'd just finished, fell asleep.

⇢⇢⇥⇤⇠⇠

HUNT LOOKED OUT the window and focused on Willowbrook Manor as they approached the front. Before the carriage came to a complete halt, the front door opened and Jenkins stood there with a smile on his face.

"Welcome home, my lord," he said when Hunt escorted the

dowager countess inside. "Lady Wickham."

"Thank you, Jenkins," Hunt said. "It's good to be home. Is His Grace in his suite?"

"Yes, my lord. As you no doubt know, His Grace has had a very trying day."

"Yes, I've heard."

Jenkins took Hunt and Lady Wickham's cloaks and handed them to a footman. "If you'll follow me, I'll show you to him."

Jenkins led the way up the stairs, and Hunt took Lady Wickham's arm and escorted her. Jenkins stopped when they reached His Grace's room. He rapped on the door, then opened it.

"Excuse me, Your Grace. You have guests."

"I don't want to see anyone, Jenkins," the duke growled.

"Oh, Your Grace. I'm sure you are eager to see *these* guests."

The Duke of Willowbrook turned his gaze to the door, and the dowager Countess of Wickham entered first.

"My lady, come in. I didn't know it was you. I'm sorry I was so—"

Hunt entered close behind, and His Grace stopped his sentence the second he looked at him.

"Hunt?" His Grace said. His voice was thick with emotion and tears formed in his eyes. "Hunt!" the duke exclaimed with excitement. He lifted his arms, and Hunt rushed into his grandfather's embrace.

Their reunion was exactly how Hunt had imagined it would be.

"When did you get home?" his grandfather asked.

"A little more than a week ago," Hunt answered.

"A little more than a week? Why didn't you come to see me?"

"I was injured. Lady Victoria found me and took me to the dowager Countess of Wickham's to recover."

"What happened to you?"

"I was shot."

The Duke of Willowbrook's features turned angry. "Did you see who shot you?"

"No."

"Was it Fridgerton or Connor?"

"I'm not sure," Hunt answered. "I assume it was one of them, though."

"Damn!" the duke shouted, then turned his gaze to the dowager countess. "I'm sorry, Genevieve."

"That's understandable, Willowbrook."

"Do you know why?" His Grace asked his grandson.

"The money, Grandfather. It might be that Connor knows if I am eliminated, he is next in line to be your heir."

"But he won't be. His father will be."

"Yes," Hunt said. "But that is the same thing. Franklin Ralston has never denied his son anything. I doubt he would in this case either."

"You are probably correct, Hunt."

Just then, Wilkins entered the room with a maid pushing a tea cart. When tea was poured and pastries served, they left the room.

"Did anyone see you arrive, Hunt?" the duke asked.

"No, Grandfather. I came in undetected."

"Good."

"Are the Ralstons still here?"

"Yes. Even Connor has returned. He met with me shortly after he left with Fridgerton and his friend."

"What did he want?" Hunt asked.

"He wanted to apologize for Fridgerton, for his rudeness to Victoria. I'm sure it was only an attempt to make sure I wasn't so angry that I would refuse him the Christmas money I always gift him and his parents. He must be deep in debt indeed if he lowered himself to grovel at my feet."

"I believe he is. And Fridgerton is probably not the only lender he is in debt to. That's why Fridgerton followed Connor here—to be the first in line to have the money he loaned Connor repaid."

"Why did Victoria not come with you?" Willowbrook asked.

Hunt looked at Lady Wickham, then he turned his gaze back to his grandfather.

"What happened to her?" Willowbrook asked in an angry voice.

"Fridgerton accosted her," Lady Wickham answered.

"Is she injured?"

"She suffered some bruises, but nothing serious. She didn't want you to see her because she knew you would be upset."

The Duke of Willowbrook leveled Hunt a serious glare. "Make him pay, Hunt. He cannot get away with laying a hand on Victoria."

"I know, Your Grace," Hunt said. "He will pay."

"You know you cannot let any of the Ralstons know you're here. As long as you're absent, they will assume the attempt on your life was successful and that you're dead."

"I know," Hunt told his grandfather. "I intend to go back to Lady Wickham's."

"And then what?" Willowbrook asked.

"Then I will take care of Fridgerton and his friend."

"Good," Willowbrook replied.

"I have a question I would like answered," Hunt said.

"What is it?" his grandfather asked.

"How did Stephen die?"

His Grace hesitated, as if it was too difficult to talk about that day. "It was a riding accident."

"Do you think it truly was an accident, Grandfather?"

"No," he announced with conviction. "Your brother was murdered. I am convinced of it."

"What are you going to do with the Ralstons?" Hunt couldn't help but ask.

"I am going to give them their Christmas money this year and tell them this is the last Christmas they will receive so much as a farthing from me. Then I will tell them I want them out of my house, and I never want to see them again. They've ruined enough Christmases with their presence, but they will ruin no more." Willowbrook turned to face Lady Wickham. "Do you think I'm being unduly harsh, Genevieve?"

"Not at all, Willowbrook," she replied. "I'm just sorry it came to this end. But they deserve their just rewards. They have spoiled their son to the point where I'm not sure he can be redeemed. It will be up to him to change his ways. If he refuses to alter his behavior, he will have to pay for his wastrel lifestyle. If even a portion of the tales about him are accurate, he is beyond redemption already."

"I feel the same, Genevieve. Are you sure Victoria was not hurt beyond a few bruises?"

"Yes, Your Grace. She is at home, and Hunter's friend Ethan is watching over her."

"Good."

Hunt stayed with his grandfather a while longer, then bade him goodbye. Jenkins led him down a back stairway of the mansion so he could escape without being seen.

Lady Wickham visited with His Grace a few minutes more, then joined Hunt in the carriage.

"You made your grandfather extremely happy, my lord," Lady Wickham said when they were on their way back to Wickham Place.

"It was good to see him so healthy."

"Yes, it was," she answered.

"Perhaps you can visit him for the next few days, my lady," Hunt suggested.

A smile brightened Lady Wickham's face. "Yes. Perhaps I can. We have always found much to talk about. We have an entire lifetime of memories to relive."

"Yes, you do. Grandfather always said there was very little about his life that you weren't a part of."

The dowager countess smiled. "That's correct. And most of it good."

"That's what Grandfather says, too."

Lady Wickham got a faraway look in her eyes and stared out

the carriage window as they traveled back to Wickham Place.

Hunt wondered what memories she was reliving. From the sly smile on her face, he was sure they were good memories. Perhaps even special memories.

CHAPTER EIGHT

WHEN THEY ARRIVED home, Hunt assisted Lady Wickham into the house, then went to find Torie. He needed to make sure she was all right. He found her reclining on a sofa in the library, reading a book.

He paused and looked at her. The three bruises on her face were darker, especially the one on her cheek below her right eye. But that wasn't what caught Hunt's attention most sharply. What stood out to him was how beautiful her features were. Her high cheekbones and kissable lips. Her long lashes and golden blonde hair. And her lush smile when she lifted her gaze to focus on him.

"How are you feeling?" he asked as he approached.

"Much better. How was your grandfather? Was he happy to see you?"

Hunt sat on the sofa next to her. "Yes. Very."

"I knew he would be." She smiled, then winced when her body told her she'd used some muscles she shouldn't have.

Hunt rose to rinse a cloth in the water on the table beside her, then placed it on the bruise darkening her cheek. "Where is Ethan?"

"He went to fill a basin with fresh water."

Hunt nodded.

"Did you manage to slip in to see your grandfather without being seen?"

"Yes."

"Was Connor there?"

"Yes. Grandfather said he'd come in to see him earlier."

"What did he want?"

"He wanted to apologize for his friends and hoped His Grace would excuse them. We know that's just an excuse to make sure Connor gets his Christmas money."

The door opened and Wilkins admitted Victoria's grandmother, followed by Ethan carrying a fresh basin of water.

"How are you feeling, Torie?" her grandmother asked.

"Much better," Victoria assured her, even though Hunt doubted that was the truth.

"Good."

Ethan placed the water next to Victoria, and Hunt rinsed a clean cloth in it then placed it on her face.

"Has she been a good patient?" Hunt asked his friend.

"Fairly good. I only had to remind her to stay still one time."

"Oh, that is good. I expected her to test you more than just once."

Everyone laughed, even Victoria. Then Wilkins entered the room and asked where Lady Wickham wanted tea served.

"Lady Victoria and our guests will take tea here, but I would like a tray sent to my room."

"Very good, my lady."

"Enjoy your tea, gentlemen," Lady Wickham said, then followed Wilkins, who held the door for her.

"Is your grandmother well?" Hunt asked.

"Yes," Victoria answered. "I suspect she's afraid you and Ethan are going to discuss plans for making Fridgerton pay for what he did, and she doesn't want to know what you intend to do."

Hunt and Ethan shared a look that indicated that was exactly what they intended to do. "And what about you, Torie?" Hunt asked. "Do you want to know our intentions?"

"I'm not sure," she answered. "I know they need to be punished, but I'm not sure I can live with their deaths on my hands. Even though it is possible Fridgerton was responsible for trying to kill you."

"And probably for killing your brother," Ethan added.

Hunt looked at his friend. "What did you discover?"

"Your brother's saddle was still in the stable, Hunt, and it's obvious that the strap had been cut. Someone wanted your brother to have an accident."

Hunt sat in stunned disbelief. It was one thing to struggle with the accidental death of a brother, but something completely different to know that Stephen's death had been intentional. To know that Stephen had been cut down in the prime of his life because of greed.

Hunt reached out and took Torie's hand in his.

She lifted her head and looked at him with tears in her eyes. "I'm so very sorry, Hunt."

"I am, too. I thought I was finished with death and killing when I left the war, but death seems to have followed me home."

"I marvel that you survived, Hunt." She turned to Ethan. "And you, Ethan. Seeing all that horrible slaughter."

Ethan answered first. "I'm not sure we did survive it, Victoria. I don't think the things we had to do, or the horror we saw, will ever leave us."

"Do you have nightmares?" she asked.

"I think we all do, my lady," Hunt said. "I think that part of war always stays with a person."

"What is different, however," Ethan added, "is that we convince ourselves that the deaths we caused were justified. We had the choice of either killing our enemy, or knowing that he would kill us. Sometimes it just came down to which one of us wanted to live more."

"Is war ever worth the loss?" she asked Hunt.

"I don't know, Torie. I don't have an answer for you."

There was silence in the room until Wilkins knocked. "Your tea tray, my lady," he announced from the doorway. Two maids pushed in a cart filled with several different kinds of pastries. One of the servants served the pastries while the other poured tea and handed cups to Hunt, Ethan, and Torie. When they were done, the servants left the room.

"Who is watching my grandfather?" Hunt asked.

"Davey," Ethan said. "I sent him back to Willowbrook to spend the night."

"Hopefully, Connor won't try anything tonight. I want to be there if and when he does. I want to be the one to make him pay. I want to hear who killed Stephen from his own mouth."

"It doesn't matter who cut the cinch," Ethan said. "Just like it doesn't matter who shot you. They were all in on it. They all had a hand in Stephen's death and your almost dying."

Hunt nodded his agreement. They'd all played a part in what happened. And they would all pay.

"Come along, Torie," Hunt said. "You need to get some rest. You're in pain. Your eyes tell me you are."

"You read me too well," Torie said. "I'm not sure I like that."

Hunt laughed. "Get used to it," he said, then helped Torie to her feet and accompanied her up the stairs and to her room. "I don't want you to know our plans. You aren't involved in what we'll do, so there's no need for you to hear them."

Hunt turned down the covers and held Torie. Then he wrapped his arms more tightly around her and brought her close. Torie lifted her gaze, and Hunt couldn't stop himself from kissing her.

When he drew back, Torie wrapped her arms around his neck and brought his mouth close to hers a second time. He nuzzled the soft outline of her lips before breaking away.

"Slide into bed and go to sleep, sweetheart. I'm sure your head hurts and you didn't get much sleep last night."

"Yes, my head hurts. And I thought I had such a hard head."

Hunt kissed her again, then pulled the covers over her when she nestled into the bed. "Come down when you wake. We'll be in the study."

He left the room and looked at her again before he closed the door behind him. This was the second time that his heart told him that he loved her.

HUNT JOINED ETHAN in the study. His friend wasted no time in broaching the subject that dominated both their thoughts.

"How do you want to handle this?"

"Fridgerton?" Hunt asked.

"Yes. Fridgerton."

"The only way he deserves to be handled. He's going to die."

"Victoria won't like it," Ethan said, but Hunt already knew that.

"No," he said, then walked to the sideboard and poured himself a glass of whiskey. He filled a glass for Ethan, took it to him, and sat. "Something tells me I'll regret killing him. When I left the war, I swore I'd never kill another human being. But something tells me I'd regret not killing these murderers even more. The man is evil. He hurt Torie, and he more than likely killed my brother. He deserves to die."

"You're right. You don't have a choice. Even if Victoria doesn't see it that way." Ethan brought his glass to his lips and took a swallow. "Before I left the service, the general called me into his office. He said he had an offer to make me."

Hunt listened with interest. "What did he want?"

"He wanted to keep me on a retainer."

"A retainer?"

"Yes, for special assignments."

"Did he explain what those special assignments would be?"

"Not in so many words, but I understood his meaning."

"What was it?"

"Evidently, my skill with a rifle had reached his ears, and he told me my particular talent would come in handy."

"He wants you to be an assassin?" Hunt whispered in disbelief. "Can you do that?"

"And live with myself?" Ethan asked.

Hunt raised an eyebrow. "Or have you already been tested?"

"I had my first assignment a week before I came here."

"And?"

Ethan took another swallow. "I hate how easy it was, Hunt. But more than that, I hate how quickly I could put what I'd done out of my mind."

Hunt sat and listened to his friend. Ethan needed to talk about what he'd done. But he didn't need anyone to condone or judge what he'd done.

"The man I was sent to eliminate was pure evil," Ethan said. "He enjoyed killing and made his victims suffer before he killed them. He especially enjoyed torturing women. I don't know how a man could be so evil."

"The authorities couldn't arrest him?"

"No one would testify against him. They were all terrified of him. He threatened to kill their families if they brought charges against him. So I eliminated him. I rid the world of a man who did not deserve to live."

"I'm not going to judge you, Ethan. I have no right to judge you. Hell, I can't even find it in me to say what you did was wrong. How can I when I killed my share of men simply because they wore the wrong color uniform?"

"Thank you, friend," Ethan said, then finished the liquor in his glass. "Someday I may give up killing."

"And when might that be?" Hunt asked.

"When I am lucky enough to meet a woman as perfect as Torie and can't face her after I've killed someone. Or when I'm asked to kill someone who doesn't deserve to die."

Ethan rose and brought the liquor decanter to his chair, then filled his and Hunt's glasses.

"Now, do you have a plan for getting rid of Fridgerton and Connor Ralston, Major?" he asked.

Hunt thought for a long moment then looked at Ethan. "I need to give myself a few more days to heal. Then you and I are going to the Willowbrook Ale House. If Fridgerton is still in the area, that's where he'll be. I'll take care of him there. Just seeing me alive should bring him out into the open. After all," Hunt added, "he thinks I'm dead. It should be quite a shock to realize I'm still alive and know what he's done."

"What do you want me to do?"

"Take care of his friend."

"I can do that," Ethan said, "although I can't promise you that I won't kill the bastard. After what he did, he deserves to die."

Hunt took a swallow from his glass. Ethan's words didn't bother him at all. He wondered what it meant when a human life was so inconsequential. But then he thought of what would have happened to Torie if Ethan hadn't stepped into the room when he did. She might have been raped. She might have been killed.

Just like Stephen had been killed.

A WEEK WENT by, and Hunt felt stronger every day. He went out riding nearly every morning and lifted anything that had weight to it, from rocks that he'd found in the drive, to half-filled bottles of brandy, to full bottles of wine. At first his arm ached from using it. Eventually, however, he scarcely noticed.

"Are you working your arms so they get stronger?" Torie asked as she entered the room where he'd been working out.

"Yes. I can't believe how weak they became just from the lack of using them."

"It doesn't take long," Torie said as she settled on a sofa to watch him.

"Too true."

Hunt lifted two wine bottles ten times each, then set them down and sat beside her on the sofa. As soon as he got comfortable, he placed his arm around her shoulders and nestled her close to him. He smiled, surprised to note how much pleasure he derived from that simple act.

"Is your grandmother visiting His Grace?"

"Yes, I asked her if she'd spend the afternoon with him so I could stay here. I had some letters to write." She was quiet for a few moments before she turned her face to him. "Aren't you going to ask me who I was going to write to?"

Hunt leaned down and kissed her forehead. "I figured if you wanted me to know, you'd tell me. Letters are private."

"Yes, they are." She turned into him and placed her head on his chest beneath his chin. "I thought I'd write to my mother and my sister. I haven't written to them since I came to stay with Grandmama."

"Did you leave them under strained conditions, Torie?"

"Yes. Father wanted to send me to an estate he owns in Scotland. But I knew if he made me go that far away, he might never allow me to return home again. So I begged him to allow me to come to stay with Grandmama. He finally agreed to let me come here on the condition that I not cause Grandmama any trouble. If I did, she has his permission to send me to Scotland."

"Trouble?" Hunt leaned away and stared at her. "I can't imagine you causing anyone any trouble."

"But I did. I caused my father a great deal of trouble."

"What did you do?"

Victoria clenched her hands in her lap and stared at them.

"Tell me, Torie."

"You'll hate me, Hunt. I know you will."

"I will not hate you. What did you do?"

"I had several very good friends. We all had our come-out Seasons together and got to know each other like sisters. One of those friends was Viscount Bradley's daughter, Frances. Viscount Bradley was deep in debt, and he sold his daughter to the highest bidder to get out of that debt."

"To whom did he sell her?"

"The Earl of Noble."

Hunt had heard of the Earl of Noble but couldn't remember what he knew about him.

"He's several years older than Frances, but not so old that she couldn't give him children. And he's very handsome. We all thought Frances was the most fortunate of us—that she had made an enviable match—and we were all so very happy for her. Then our happiness faded."

Hunt remembered what he'd heard about Noble and knew Torie's story was going to turn into a nightmare.

"Not that long after they were married, the earl started coming to social events without Frances. When we asked about her, he hinted that she wasn't feeling well. At first we thought she might be with child, which was the reason she wasn't well. Then we realized that wasn't the case. She didn't attend functions because she stayed home to hide the bruises Noble gave her.

"One night Frances came to my house. She was terrified to be alone with her husband. Noble had beaten her so severely she could barely move. I knew she couldn't stay with him any longer, or the next time he'd kill her. I collected all the money I had. I hired a driver and put her on a ship going to Boston."

Torie clasped her fingers tighter in her lap and squeezed them until her knuckles turned white. "She escaped, but Noble discovered that I had helped her flee from him. He came to our house and was furious. I wouldn't tell him where she was."

"What did your father do?"

"The only thing he could do. It was against the law for anyone to help a wife escape from her husband." Torie reached for her glass of wine and drank a large portion of it. "Noble petitioned for a divorce from Frances on the grounds of adultery. Lord Noble demanded repayment of the money he'd given Frances' father for marriage to his daughter, which Viscount Bradley didn't have. Frances' family was ruined and her father put in debtor's prison."

"Is he still there?"

"I think so."

Victoria's eyes filled with tears, and the first of many ran down her cheeks.

"And that is why your father sent you away," Hunt said.

Victoria nodded. "As soon as word got out that I had helped Frances escape, members of the *ton* were furious. If I escaped punishment for what I'd done, what was to stop others from doing the same thing?"

Hunt wiped away tears he saw streaming down her cheeks.

"Father was left with no choice but to banish me. I'm just fortunate that Grandmama intervened and took me in."

Hunt gathered her close and held her until her tears subsided.

"Now you know what I've done and why it's not safe for you to care for me," she said. "I'm headstrong and devious."

"Do you think I care?"

"You have to, Hunt."

Hunt laughed. "You saved my life, Victoria. What kind of man would I be if I abandoned you for saving your friend?"

"Oh, Hunt," she said, then turned into him and tilted her face until her lips met his.

Their kiss was laced with passion. Hunt opened his mouth atop hers and deepened his kiss. When they couldn't breathe any longer, Hunt broke the kiss and gathered her to him until they calmed.

"What are you going to do about Fridgerton?" she asked.

"Don't worry, Torie. I will handle this. It's my problem. He killed my brother."

She snuggled against him and breathed a deep sigh. He wasn't sure if she realized what he intended to do. If she didn't, it was because she chose not to know. And that was fine.

She had a very soft heart. That was one of the most special things about her. One of the reasons he loved her.

CHAPTER NINE

HUNT SAT AT a table toward the back of the ale room in the Willowbrook Ale House with Ethan at his side. He watched who entered the pub each time the door opened, hoping it would be Fridgerton and his friend. He wanted to get this behind him. He wanted to make Fridgerton pay for the pain he'd inflicted on Torie. He wanted to make Fridgerton pay for the bullet he'd put in his shoulder. He wanted Fridgerton to pay for the part he'd played in Stephen's death.

"How much longer are we going to wait?" Ethan asked, after the barmaid delivered another ale to their table.

"A little longer. The barmaid said Fridgerton and his friend come every night and stay until closing."

Hunt lifted the tankard but stopped midway to his mouth. The alehouse door opened and Fridgerton and his friend entered. They hadn't taken more than three steps into the room when they froze and glared at Hunt and Ethan.

"Do you think they recognized us?" Ethan said sarcastically.

"Oh, yes. Yes indeed."

Hunt waited to see what they would do. Fridgerton glared at Hunt. This was the first time Fridgerton had seen him since he'd put a bullet in his shoulder. It was obvious he was surprised to see Hunt alive. And he was immediately on his guard.

Fridgerton gave Hunt his back and stepped to the bar to order an ale. The bartender filled two tankards, and when Fridgerton turned, Hunt caught his attention.

"Would you care to join us?" Hunt asked. "I feel as if we're old friends. We do have a past, you know."

Fridgerton hesitated, then walked to Hunt and Ethan, where he and his friend pulled out two chairs and sat.

"We finally meet," Hunt said. "I always feel better when I've met the man who tried to kill me."

Fridgerton slid back his chair and reached for what Hunt assumed was a gun.

"Don't even try," he said before Fridgerton could pull the gun from his vest. "I have a pistol aimed at your gut, and I won't hesitate to use it. In fact, I will *enjoy* using it."

"What do you want?" Fridgerton asked in a threatening tone.

"First, I want to know why you tried to kill me and who put you up to it."

"That should be obvious," Fridgerton said with a snide smile.

"It is," Hunt answered. "But I want to hear you say it."

"Ralston."

"Which Ralston?"

Fridgerton laughed. "The boy. Connor. He has a nasty gambling habit, which wouldn't be any different than most of Society, if he had the luck to go with it. But he doesn't. He has no luck at all, and he owes me more than he'll ever be able to pay. Unless, of course, he can get his hands on a great deal of wealth."

"And with me dead—"

"He's one step closer to inheriting the Willowbrook fortune."

"What about His Grace? He's still alive."

"And he'll remain alive for another week. At least until Christmas Day, when Willowbrook gives the Ralstons their Christmas gifts. That will be my first payment. The rest will come when His Grace is dead, and Connor's father becomes the next Willowbrook."

"Which won't happen now. As you see, I'm still alive, and Ralston is one step further from all that wealth."

Fridgerton laughed. "Which leaves you standing on very thin ice, Murdock. It's in my best interest to eliminate you, something I should have taken care of before, instead of leaving it up to that snot-nosed kid. But Connor swore he could handle it. He wanted to pull the trigger himself. I should have known better." Fridgerton reached for his ale and took a large gulp. "If that's all, Murdock, I'd like to drink my ale without having to look at your miserable face."

"No, there is one more issue I'd like to discuss."

"What?"

Hunt stood. "Not in here. This is a private matter." He made sure Fridgerton realized he had his gun close to hand.

"And if I refuse?"

"I don't remember giving you that choice. Now, move."

Fridgerton rose from his chair and walked to the door. Ethan was there first, and held the door while Fridgerton exited, with Hunt close behind him.

When they reached the center of the drive, Fridgerton turned. Before he had time to lift his hands, Hunt pulled back his arm and rammed his fist into Fridgerton's jaw. Fridgerton landed on his arse on the stone drive.

"That's for Lady Victoria," Hunt said. He waited long enough for Fridgerton to get to his feet, then struck him again.

Fridgerton struggled to his feet a second time, and Hunt hit him again. Then again. And again.

After the fifth time, the coward didn't try to get to his feet. Blood ran from his nose, mouth, and a cut above his eye.

Hunt stood over him with his legs wide and his fists anchored at his hips, and glared at the coward. "If you ever dare to come near her again, I'll kill you. Do you understand?"

"Yes," Fridgerton slurred through his cut lips.

"Now, get the hell back to London before I decide you need another lesson." Hunt turned and glared at Fridgerton's friend. "Get this worthless pile of dung out of my sight."

Fridgerton's friend ran to where Fridgerton lay crumpled on

the ground. He tried to lift the bloodied man, but even as Fridgerton struggled to his feet, he pulled out his gun.

Hunt spun to the side. Fridgerton's shot went wide. Hunt fired a return shot that hit Fridgerton in the center of his forehead. He fell backward, dead even before he hit the ground.

"You killed him," a bystander from the inn cried out. "Good for you."

"I saw the whole thing," another bystander yelled.

"It was self-defense," another man yelled. "The dead bloke fired first."

"Come on," Ethan said, patting Hunt on the back. "Let's go in and wait for the constable to get here. I'm sure this won't take long."

Hunt stretched his shoulders. His arm ached from overexerting it, but it was worth every jolt of pain. All he had to do was remember that he'd never see his brother again because of Fridgerton, and envision the bruises on Torie's face, and it was more than worth it.

Hunt and Ethan returned to the ale room and sat at a table to await the constable. So much for keeping a low profile. So much for not making a scene. By morning, what he'd done would be all over town. Torie and her grandmother would hear about it whether he wanted them to or not.

Hunt ordered another ale, then paid for a round for the patrons who'd gathered. They'd be the ones who would relate what had happened to the constable. They deserved the round.

"You know who will be happiest about Fridgerton's death?" Ethan said before taking a drink of his ale.

"Yes," Hunt answered. "Connor Ralston. We just eliminated the man he owed more money than he'd ever be able to repay."

Ethan nodded. "Yes. You did him one hell of a favor."

"I would have if Fridgerton were the only lender he borrowed money from. But I have a feeling there's a whole pack of money lenders waiting in line to collect from Ralston."

"He's in a whole pile of trouble, then," Ethan said as they

waited for the constable to come to their table.

This was going to be a very long night.

TORIE WOKE THE next morning to the sun streaming through her window. It had been nearly a week since Hunt's altercation with the now-deceased Fridgerton. She and Grandmama had heard about it before breakfast the morning after it happened, but Hunt wasn't the person who told them. It was the main topic of conversation among all the servants in both Wickham Place and Willowbrook Estate. It was all anyone talked about. It seemed Hunt had proven his bravery, and Fridgerton was shown to be the coward everyone knew he was.

Torie waited for Hunt to tell her what had happened, or at least mention it in passing, but he didn't. He ignored it as if it had never happened. She knew one day she would have to bring up the subject. Or maybe she never would.

For the second week in December, it was beautiful outside. The only complaint she had was that there was no snow on the ground, which made it feel less like Christmas.

She threw the covers off and carried out her morning ablutions, then chose a gown to wear as her lady's maid entered the room.

"Is Lady Wickham up yet?" she asked Stomes.

"Yes, my lady. She's in the dining room with Lord Murdock and Mr. Essex."

"Lord Murdock and Mr. Essex are here?"

"Yes, miss. I believe they came to see if you and the dowager would like to go into the village.

"Oh, I would love to. But that means I'm late."

Stomes laughed. "Or they are early."

Torie laughed too. Oh, this was going to be a perfect day. She'd been anxious to go to Willowbrook Village. She'd heard there was a new restaurant that had opened next to the bakery. She would love to have lunch there. A tobacco shop had recently opened where she hoped to replenish the Duke of Willowbrook's leather pouch, and word of a new milliner on Trowbridge Street had her intrigued. Grandmama said that Willowbrook Village was growing faster than the cobblestone layers could keep up with.

But the one thing they still desperately needed was a physician. They only had a midwife. They needed a real doctor. Perhaps what they should do is advertise in the *London Times*. That might entice a doctor to move to the country. Torie would have to mention her idea to Grandmama. She could also discuss it with His Grace, and perhaps they could send an advertisement to the paper yet this week.

Victoria hurried to the dining room to find her grandmama, Hunt, and Ethan already seated at the table.

"Good morning," she said. When the men rose, she held out her hand to stop them. "There's no need to rise. Your food will get cold."

Torie went to the breakfast buffet and filled her plate. When she returned, a footman helped her sit.

"You gentlemen are up and about early this morning," Torie teased.

"Yes, we explained to your grandmother that when we stepped out, we realized it was a perfect day to tour the town," Hunt said.

"That's a wonderful idea. Grandmama has told me about all the new shops and stores that have opened. Willowbrook is quite the growing village."

"At this rate," the dowager countess quipped, "we will have outgrown the status of *village*."

"That's exciting," Torie said. "I was just thinking this morning, though, that the one thing Willowbrook still needs is a doctor."

"Yes," everyone agreed.

"How does one go about getting a doctor?" Hunt asked. "We can't just wait around for one to show up, can we?"

"No," Torie said. "We have to advertise. We need to put an advertisement in the *London Times* stating that the town of Willowbrook is looking for a physician. Perhaps we might even write a letter to a well-known doctor in London to ask for suggestions. We definitely want a reputable physician who can care for the citizens of Willowbrook."

"That's a wonderful idea," Hunt said, reaching over to squeeze Torie's fingers.

At his touch, a sizzling shot of heat surged through her body. She'd experienced something similar when she walked into the dining room earlier and saw him sitting at the table. What was it about the sight of him that caused every nerve in her body to come alive?

"Does Willowbrook have a bookshop?" Ethan asked.

"A bookshop?" Hunt asked.

"Yes. My father owns a bookshop in London. He also carries stationery supplies, and a variety of writing implements, newspapers, and a few assorted gifts."

Hunt looked at his friend. "I didn't know that about you, Ethan. You never mentioned your father's business."

"There's a lot about me that I haven't mentioned."

"Like what?"

"That I enjoy reading, for instance. And writing."

"Writing?"

"Yes. Especially children's stories."

"That's fascinating, Ethan. Why haven't you ever mentioned this before?"

"And have the soldiers in our division laugh at me?" Ethan asked. "And you know they would have."

"Yes, probably," Hunt replied. "They would have found it humorous to know that the soldier with the reputation for being the best shot in our division, and with the most kill shots, writes books for babies."

"Well, I think it's remarkable," Victoria said, looking at the embarrassment on Ethan's face. "I think you should find someone to illustrate your stories and get them published. Then sell them in your father's store in London, and your own store in Willowbrook."

Ethan laughed. "Has anyone ever told you that you are a dreamer, my lady?"

"Many times. And if I could draw, I would illustrate your stories and help you get them printed myself. But painting is not something I'm good at."

"Well, this is enough dreaming for one day," Hunt said. "Let's get our cloaks and head for Willowbrook. We'll check to see if there's a book store, and if not, we'll look for a perfect spot for one. Right, my friend?" He clapped Ethan on the back, and they shared a hearty laugh.

On that happy note, they all rose from the table and went to the foyer to get their coats and hats and gloves. When they were ready to go out, they got into the Wickham carriage and headed to town. It didn't take them long to reach the main road through Willowbrook. They disembarked from the carriage and leisurely strolled down the board-covered paths.

As they made their way through the growing village, she thought of several improvements she might suggest. First, she would have all the village walkways changed from boards to brick. With each idea that came to her, Torie grew more excited. She could imagine several ways she and Hunt could help Willowbrook grow into a modern city.

Not only did Willowbrook need more shops and stores, but it also needed a place for entertainment. A concert hall, or theatre, for plays and operas. And a park—an area where people could go to picnic and stroll on a Sunday afternoon. And a promenade. Just like London had Hyde Park, Willowbrook needed Willowbrook Park. She would bring that up the next time they visited with the Duke of Willowbrook. He'd paid for a majority of the businesses that were awaiting shop owners to purchase them. Torie was sure he would pay for a large portion of land to be cordoned off for a park.

Oh, there were several more important areas that needed to be built to make their town an inviting place for people to move to. She couldn't wait to share her ideas with His Grace. And her grandmother. And Hunt.

VICTORIA AND HER grandmother walked side by side along the streets of Willowbrook. They saw several new shops that had opened since the last time they were here, and stopped in to see what they offered. Torie's grandmother made several purchases, and Torie even bought an item or two. She made a point of not spending too much money, since she had none of her own and had to rely on her grandmother to pay for her purchases.

She did see a bonnet she desperately wanted, but refused to ask her grandmother for it. Torie was disappointed when her grandmother purchased the bonnet for herself. It was so pretty— pale purple with lavender and white lilacs circling the brim, and matching purple ribbons that would tie beneath her chin. Indeed, it was her grandmother's color, and she couldn't begrudge how prettily it would complement the dowager's lovely silver hair.

Torie watched as the store clerk put the bonnet in a box and handed it to her grandmother. She prayed that she might be allowed to wear it herself once or twice.

As they were getting ready to leave the milliner's, Hunt and Ethan entered. "Did you find a bookshop?" Torie asked.

"No," Hunt answered. "But we haven't searched down this street yet."

"Then let's do it together," Torie said. "Would one of you gentlemen carry Grandmama's purchases?" she asked, then handed the bonnet to Ethan when he held out his hands.

"The carriage is close by," he said. "I'll carry these purchases to the carriage. It won't take me but a minute."

"We'll walk slowly," Torie said, knowing that her grandmother was probably getting tired.

They left the milliner's shop and started walking down the street. They hadn't gone far at all before a man exited a shop and walked toward them. The moment he saw Torie, then Hunt, he stopped short.

"Well, Lord Murdock," Connor Ralston said. "What a shock to see you."

"To see me?" Hunt said. "Or to realize that you didn't kill me, and I am still alive?"

"Now, now, Murdock. I have no idea what you are implying. I assure you that I have nothing but the best wishes for you and His Grace."

"You leave His Grace out of your thoughts."

"My, my. You are indeed touchy."

"I get that way when someone tries to kill me," Hunt said.

Connor's lips narrowed and lifted at the corners in a snide grin. "Surely, you don't think I had anything to do with your mishap."

"I know you did. Just as I know you are responsible for my brother's death. And when I can prove it, I'll see you hang."

"You'll never be able to prove it," Connor boasted.

"I'd be very careful if I were you, Ralston. Fridgerton and I had a very interesting conversation the other night. It's amazing what information someone will volunteer when persuaded to talk."

The grin faded from Connor's face. "Rumor has it that my friend Fridgerton can no longer offer any information, since he is reported to be dead."

"Perhaps he is, cousin. But Mr. Fridgerton and I had a very interesting conversation before he died. He told me some very fascinating facts I had previously only surmised. The point is," Hunt said, taking another step closer to Connor, "you are on your own now, cousin. And that should frighten you immensely."

Just then, Ethan joined them. "Well, Hunt," he said. "Look who crawled out from beneath a rock."

"Yes, but I think he was just about to crawl back into his hole."

Connor issued Hunt and Ethan an icy glare, then strode past them to his waiting horse.

"Be careful of him, Hunt. He's dangerous," Ethan warned.

Torie reached for Hunt's hand and clenched his fingers. She needed to tell him, if not in words then at least by touch, that she was worried for him.

He looped her arm through his and began to walk down the street. "Come, ladies. Let's find that bookshop. This is the last street we have to investigate. If we don't find it, at least there's a nice-looking restaurant at the end of the walk. I'll treat you all to lunch."

"I can't wait," Torie's grandmother said. "I'm quite hungry."

"Me too," Ethan said, leading the dowager countess toward the restaurant.

Torie and Hunt let Ethan and the dowager countess walk ahead of them. "Do be careful, Hunt," Torie said. "Connor Ralston isn't someone to take lightly."

"I know, Victoria. I just survived a war. I'm not about to allow a single untrained coward to kill me."

"I know, but this untrained coward doesn't fight fairly."

"Not to worry, my lady. I know every trick in the book," Hunt said, then led Torie into the restaurant and found them a table.

A young girl with a sunny face came to the table to ask what they would like to order. When the girl left to relay their order to the kitchen, an older woman came to the table.

"Lady Wickham," she said. "It's such a pleasure to have you join us."

"Rosann," the dowager countess responded. "Please, allow me to introduce my guests. This," she said, indicating Hunt, "is Lord Murdock, the Duke of Willowbrook's grandson."

"My lord," Rosann said, bobbing politely.

"And this is my granddaughter, Lady Victoria Crawley. She has come to stay with me for however long I can convince her to remain."

"My lady," Rosann greeted Torie, bobbing again.

"And this is Mr. Ethan Essex, a friend of Lord Murdock's. They served in the army together."

"Mr. Essex. It's a pleasure to meet all of you. I'm honored that you have joined us today."

"Perhaps you could answer a question for me," Torie said. "Does Willowbrook have a bookshop, by chance?"

"No, I'm afraid we don't, although we are in desperate need of one. Willowbrook has seen several new businesses start up lately, but none of them have been a bookshop, and I know one would be very popular."

"I think so, too," Torie said.

Before more could be said, their meals arrived and the owner of the restaurant excused herself.

"See, Ethan?" Torie said. "You would be filling a need in Willowbrook. Are you serious about opening a bookshop?"

"I'd have to speak with my father before I do anything permanent, but there's nothing I'd like more."

"If you're concerned about money, don't be," Hunt told his friend. "I will underwrite your project."

"And you must allow me to assist with the funding also," the dowager countess said. "I would be privileged to help out."

Torie was moved by how brightly Ethan's smile shone.

"I don't know what to say. Thank you. But I have put quite a nest egg aside."

"Well, if you need anything at all, don't hesitate to ask. It will be worth it to have my best friend so close," Hunt said.

They finished their meals on a happy note, then located their carriage waiting nearby. Torie had a lot to think over. Even though Hunt wasn't concerned about Connor, she was. He'd already tried to kill Hunt once, and nothing was stopping him from trying again.

Even though Hunt hadn't mentioned what happened to Fridgerton, now she knew that Fridgerton was dead. She should have known. He'd disappeared too conveniently, and the fact that neither Hunt nor Ethan had mentioned him of late was an obvious sign that they were not worried about him—because he was no longer a threat.

But Connor was. He was desperate for the Willowbrook money, and the only way he could get his hands on it was to eliminate Hunt, then the Duke of Willowbrook.

Connor Ralston had come too far now to stop. He'd already had a hand in killing Hunt's brother and in shooting Hunt. There was only one possible ending for this tragedy. One of them would die. But would it be Connor? Or Hunt?

CHAPTER TEN

I T TOOK A lot of talking to convince Hunt to stay at Wickham House rather than go back to Willowbrook Manor, but Hunt finally gave in to Torie's pleading arguments that he would be safer here. And she was probably correct. Now that Connor knew his plan to kill him hadn't worked, he wasn't safe anywhere.

The one good thing that came out of Hunt's decision to stay there was that it forced his grandfather to get out of bed and take the ducal carriage the short distance to Wickham Place to see Hunt. There were days that the Duke of Willowbrook spent the entire day at Wickham Place. Hunt enjoyed those days the most. They were leading up to a perfect Christmas, and after three years fighting the war, this would be the first real Christmas he'd had in a long time.

The only problem he had was that although he was safer at Wickham House than at Willowbrook Manor, it wasn't forcing Connor to show his hand. It was simply postponing the inevitable.

Hunt spent hours devising a plan that would force Connor into the open, but the only plan he could come up with involved a certain amount of risk, and that was something Victoria would see right through.

"Is Connor back at Willowbrook Manor?" he asked his grandfather when he'd arrived to spend the day.

"Yes, he moved back in. I think he thought I wouldn't notice, but my staff is so loyal that they keep me informed of everything that goes on in my house."

"Good."

"Why do you need to know, Hunt?" Torie asked, looking up from the book she was reading.

"I just think it's wise to know where he is. Ethan has been searching for a location for his bookshop, and he thinks he's found one. He wants me to go with him to check it over, and I said I would."

"Do you think that's wise?"

"Torie," he said, moving to sit beside her. He reached for her hand and held it. "Nothing I do will be wise as long as Connor is still desperate for my inheritance."

"Maybe he doesn't want the money so badly that he would kill you for it," Torie said. "He knows we're already aware of his involvement in the last attempt. Maybe he'll just cut his losses and run."

The Duke of Willowbrook laughed, and Hunt smiled.

"That's hardly possible, Torie. It's an astronomical amount. Far too large for Connor to ignore."

"There isn't a man alive addicted to gambling," the Duke of Willowbrook added, "who will ever have enough money. He will always want more."

"How are you going to stop him?" she asked, refusing to look away from Hunt. She studied him, expecting him to answer her truthfully.

"Whatever I have to do, Torie."

She shook her head. "No, Hunt."

"I don't have a choice. Not if I want a future."

"But—"

Torie was stopped from finishing her thought when the door opened and Ethan entered the room.

"Ethan," Hunt said. "You're just in time. Sit down and tell us about the location you found."

Ethan broke into a huge smile. "It's the perfect spot," he said, sitting in the chair next to Hunt. "I can't wait for you to see it."

"And you want to go now?" Hunt asked.

"Yes, if you don't mind."

"Not at all." Hunt turned to Torie. "Would you like to come with us?"

"Of course," she answered. "Just let me run up and get my cloak."

"Very well. We'll wait for you in the foyer."

"Help me on your way up the stairs, would you, Torie?" the duke asked.

"Of course, Your Grace," she replied. "It's time for you to rest."

"Yes, I'm getting a little tired."

Hunt watched his grandfather and Torie leave the room, then turned to Ethan.

"What is it?" he asked.

"How do you know I have something to tell you?"

"We've known each other too long for you to pretend ignorance, Ethan. What is it?"

"Connor is in Willowbrook."

"You saw him?"

"Yes. He was just entering Willowbrook when I was leaving."

"This could happen sooner than I thought it might. I wish Torie wasn't going with us."

"So do I," Ethan said. "I wouldn't want her to get caught up in this."

Just then, Torie entered the room with her cloak on.

"Will you be warm enough?" Hunt asked.

She smiled. "I'll be fine. It isn't that cold in this part of England. We aren't that far north. Now, if we were closer to Scotland…" she said to Ethan as they walked from the room and out the front door.

Ethan escorted her to the carriage while Hunt went to his room and put a pistol in his pocket. He hoped he wouldn't need it, but it was better to be safe than sorry.

"OH, ETHAN," TORIE said when she entered the vacant building Ethan had found for his bookshop. "This is perfect. It's like it was built to be a bookshop."

"Do you think so?" he asked, walking through the building.

"Oh, yes!" she answered.

"And the location is perfect," Hunt added. "Close enough to the main thoroughfare where most of the people shopping for hats and gloves and ribbons and scarves will come, yet isolated enough that it has a special feel to it."

"That's what I thought, too." Ethan walked behind the counter. "And there are enough shelves that I won't have to add too many more. All they'll need is a coat of paint."

"And the windows are wide enough that you'll have a great deal of display room. And that will let in a lot of light."

"Yes," Ethan said, as if that wasn't something he'd considered.

"Have you spoken to whoever owns the building?" Hunt asked.

"No, not yet. I'm told that Baron Darling owns this property. Do you know him?"

"No, I'm afraid I don't, but maybe His Grace does."

"Well, it doesn't matter. Although I'm set on purchasing this particular property, it's not as if it's the only vacant storefront in Willowbrook. If I can't get this location, I'll find another."

"That's a perfect way to think about it," Torie said.

She watched as Hunt stepped to the door and stared out the window. This was the third or fourth time he'd looked outside. It was as if he was watching for something or someone.

"And there's a quaint little sandwich and tea shop two doors down the street," Ethan said. "I had lunch there the other day, and it was quite good."

"Oh, perfect. At least we know you'll never go hungry," Torie teased.

"What do you think, Major?"

Hunt took a glance out the window again then turned to face his friend. "What did you say?"

"I asked what you thought. Do you agree this is perfect?"

Hunt stepped back into the shop and looked around. "I think it's perfect. The location is ideal, and there seems to be a good amount of room for any number of books, stationery supplies, and anything else you decide to sell."

"I wonder how much Baron Darling would want for this property."

While Ethan and Hunt were discussing other possibilities for the bookshop, Torie walked to the door and stared out the window to see what Hunt could have been looking at. Just then, the door to the Willowbrook Ale House on the opposite corner opened and two men exited.

Torie thought she recognized one of the men, but he was so far away she couldn't be sure. It wasn't until they took several steps toward her that she was certain.

The man was Connor Ralston.

A painful rock fell to the pit of her stomach. The two men were arguing. She was sure they were by their sharp hand gestures and angry facial expressions.

She cast a glance at Hunter, but he was still in deep conversation with Ethan and didn't notice her.

Torie wrapped her arms around her waist and clenched her fists. Her breath caught and she struggled to stay calm. She turned back to Hunt, and this time his gaze locked with hers.

"Torie?" he asked.

She shook her head. She didn't want him to ask her what was wrong, and she knew if he said anything, that was the question he would ask. Torie was sure there was terror etched across her face that made the fear she felt obvious.

Hunt walked toward her, then stood at the window and

looked across the street. With a grimace, he pulled her into his arms and held her.

"It's all right, Torie. They don't know I'm here."

"But Connor has someone with him. That means you aren't safe any longer."

"I've never been safe. Not since they decided to kill me."

"Do you know who the other man is?" Torie asked. "Maybe he's someone Connor hired to kill you."

"No. From the way they're arguing, the man is no doubt another money lender that Connor owes."

"What are we going to do?"

"Nothing. Don't worry, Torie. I'm safe as long as I'm in public. I'm the grandson of the Duke of Willowbrook. The namesake of this community. If they attempt to harm me in public, they will both be charged with murder. Even Connor isn't that foolish."

Torie wrapped her arms around Hunt and pressed her cheek to his chest. His heart had a steady beat, while Torie's was thundering in her chest. How could he remain so calm? She was terrified. She thought back to the afternoon she'd found him bleeding on the floor of the cottage. And she didn't even know him then. He was a stranger. Not the man she loved.

"Come, sweetheart," Hunt said. "Let's get you home. You've had enough excitement for one day."

"Perhaps we should remain inside a little longer, just in case they haven't left yet."

"I'm sure they're gone, Torie," Hunt said, clearly wanting to reassure her. Thankfully, though, Ethan came up with an idea that seemed to solve their problem.

"Why don't you and Victoria stay here, and I'll go for the carriage?" Ethan suggested.

"Yes," Torie said with a sigh of relief.

"I'll be right back," Ethan said, then left the building.

"How can you be so calm?" Torie said, knowing she sounded as if she was scolding Hunt.

"Perhaps it's because of my time in Her Majesty's army. If I fell apart every time I went into battle, I'd be dead by now."

"Oh, Hunt," Torie said through the first wave of tears.

Instead of gently holding her like she wanted him to, Hunt clasped her shoulders and roughly pulled her to him. He brought his mouth down on hers and kissed her. His kiss wasn't soft or gentle, and it dominated with a strength that stole her breath.

He tilted her head to help him gain better access, then deepened his kiss. His kisses contained more fervor and passion than Torie was equipped to handle. His tongue skimmed her lips then forced them to open to accept his intrusion.

Again and again he kissed her, brutally forcing her to match his desire. Her legs weakened, and Torie hung on to him to keep her balance—and to keep from crumpling to the floor.

He tightened his hold on her while he kissed her again. Then, in a startling move, he broke their kiss and crushed her to his chest. He held her for several long seconds while they each panted to catch their breath.

"Are you all right?" he asked. "Did I hurt you?"

"No," she said in a whisper. "I am fine."

He ran his hand down her back. "I love you," he said in a matter-of-fact tone, as if it was important that she knew how he felt about her. "I love that you are worried about me. That you look out for my wellbeing and safety. No one has ever worried about me like you do. All my time in the army, I was in charge of looking out for the soldiers beneath me. No one was in charge of watching over me."

"Oh, Hunt," she sighed, and held on to him a little tighter

He was as frightened as she was. He simply had a different way of showing it. He reacted to fear with violence, where Torie reacted to it with tears.

She cupped her hand to his cheek and tilted his head toward her, then kissed him several more times until Ethan arrived with the carriage. Only then was she forced to release him.

CONNOR RALSTON STARED at Liam Nixon with the most lethal glare he could muster. Even though he was shaking inside, he couldn't let Nixon know how afraid he was of his threats. He wouldn't survive if he did. Hell, there was every possibility that he wouldn't survive even if Nixon didn't realize how afraid he was.

Nixon was one of the most feared money lenders in all of London. Connor should have known better than to go to him for money, but Fridgerton had been breathing down his neck. He didn't have a choice.

He swore he would never get in this position again. From now on, he wouldn't bet more money than he could cover. He'd never write another IOU in his life. That was what got him in trouble this time—thinking that luck was with him when it wasn't. Thinking he was going to win when he wasn't. Thinking that this time he was going to strike it rich, when he wasn't. If only Willowbrook had helped him out.

He'd gone to the Duke of Willowbrook and as much as begged him for an early Christmas present. He needed the money the duke always handed out on Christmas morning *now*. Maybe that would've pacified Nixon for at least a few weeks. But right now he had to get himself out of this mess. And there was only one thing that would save him—he had to get his hands on the Willowbrook inheritance. He had to kill Hunter Melbourne, Earl of Murdock, then kill the Duke of Willowbrook.

"When will I get my money, Ralston?" Nixon asked.

"As soon as I get it from Willowbrook. I told you, he pays us every Christmas. He calls it our Christmas present."

"How much will you get?"

Connor thought of the amount he usually got, then added the amount his parents usually shelled out to him as his Christmas present from them, then doubled the total.

"That doesn't come close to what you owe me," Nixon bellowed. "You know what happens to people who fail to pay their debts," he threatened. "They live very short lives."

"You'll get your money. I just have to eliminate Murdock."

"That still doesn't get you next in line to Willowbrook's money," Nixon told him.

"I know. I know."

"Then you have to eliminate His Grace," Nixon reminded him. "And then your father."

Connor swallowed hard. He hadn't considered killing his father. He wasn't sure he could do that. Surely when his father inherited the title he would be generous with his son and killing him would not be necessary.

"Do you understand?" Nixon demanded.

"Yes. Yes. I understand. I'll get it done," Connor said.

"Soon."

"Yes, soon."

Connor watched Nixon walk away and tried to keep his stomach from getting rid of the little he'd eaten today. He knew better than to ignore Nixon's threats.

Connor was more terrified of Nixon than he was of Fridgerton. The man didn't issue vacant threats. He carried them. Or one of his minions did.

His blood ran cold. He was afraid he was a dead man.

CHAPTER ELEVEN

HUNT HAD BEEN forced to remain indoors for nearly an entire week. That was as long as he could stand. He was going mad staying inside.

He put his pistol in his jacket pocket and walked across the foyer to the front door.

"Are you going out?" Torie asked as he put on his outer coat.

"I promised Ethan I'd go with him when he met with his solicitor. He talked to Baron Darling, and they came to an agreement on a selling price. I told him I'd cosign the note and they could proceed with the sale. After today, Ethan will be the proud owner of his own bookshop."

"Oh, that's wonderful."

"Yes. He's quite excited about having his own business."

"I don't blame him. Would you like me to accompany you?" Torie asked.

"Would you like to?"

"If you don't mind. I'd love to."

"Of course I don't mind." Hunt turned to the butler. "Wilkins, please have someone bring the carriage around."

"Right away, my lord."

Hunt led Torie to the ground floor's sitting room to wait until the carriage arrived. "Is your grandmother visiting my grandfather?"

"Yes. He invited her for lunch in the solarium." Torie chuckled. "They've been spending a great deal of time together lately, don't you think?"

"Yes, but I'm glad. His Grace has never been happier."

"Nor Grandmama."

Wilkins came to the door and announced that the carriage was ready and waiting out front. Hunt escorted Torie into the carriage, and they made their way into Willowbrook Village.

"Where are you to meet Ethan?" Torie asked.

"At the bookshop."

They drove to the bookshop, and Hunt helped Torie to the street.

"Is everyone here?" Hunt asked when they entered the building.

"Everyone except Baron Darling," Ethan answered. "His solicitor expects him at any moment."

Just then, Baron Darling arrived. He walked through the door and stopped short when he saw Victoria.

"Lady Victoria," he said. "Imagine meeting you here."

"Baron Darling," Torie greeted him.

"Are you acquainted?" Hunt asked.

"Yes. Lady Victoria's father and I are close friends. The Earl of Wickham and I are involved in several ventures together."

"Allow me to introduce myself," Hunt said. "Hunter Melbourne, Earl of Murdock."

"That would make you the Duke of Willowbrook's—"

"—only remaining grandson," Hunt said, setting the boundaries right away.

"Yes, well. I should have known Willowbrook was involved in this. The town is named after him, after all."

"Yes, it is," Hunt said. "That's because he has done more than anyone else to make sure Willowbrook thrives and grows. The shops that are now standing are here because Willowbrook either built them himself, or encouraged men like yourself to build them so that potential shop owners can find an ideal spot already built. Just as Ethan has."

"Yes," Ethan agreed. "Having the building ready to occupy makes starting a business so much easier."

"Now, should we proceed?" Baron Darling's solicitor said, gathering his papers and sorting them.

Hunt noticed that Torie had found a stool to sit on. The color had drained from her face. She'd clenched her hands in her lap the second Baron Darling walked into the shop and recognized her. He knew what had happened to her, and it wouldn't be long before all of London Society knew that she'd escaped to her grandmother's.

The business at hand regained his attention, and it didn't take long before all the papers were signed, and the transaction was completed. Then Baron Darling and the two solicitors moved to the door. The solicitors left first, but Darling stopped before he stepped out of the building.

"Lady Victoria," he said, turning to face her. "If you ever come into contact with Frances Bradley—"

"Since I don't know Frances Bradley's specific whereabouts, and she does not know mine, I doubt I shall come into contact with her," Torie interrupted.

"Well, if you *should* ever come into contact with her, would you please extend my heartfelt sympathies to her upon the death of her husband?"

"The Earl of Noble is dead?"

"Yes. Quite unfortunate. He was set upon by a gang of ruffians and killed. It was quite confusing. Everyone assumed it was a robbery gone wrong, yet nothing was taken from his person."

"How was he killed?" Hunt asked.

"He was beaten to death. Quite gruesome."

Victoria brought her hand up to cover her gasp.

"Some say it was a form of poetic justice, whatever that means," Darling said. "Well, Lord Murdock, Mr. Essex, my lady. It was a pleasure doing business with you. And good luck with your bookshop, Mr. Essex."

"It was a pleasure," Ethan said as Darling walked out the door.

The minute they were alone, Hunt stepped over to where Torie was sitting and wrapped his arm around her. "Obviously, he abused someone else, and this time the lady's family objected to how she was treated."

"Do you think they hired thugs to kill him?" Torie asked.

"Probably. We'll no doubt never know." Hunt lifted Torie's head to look her in the eye. "*Do* you know where she is?"

She shook her head. "Although her brother might. He helped me get her out of London. I told him I didn't want to know so that if ever I was asked, I could say with all honesty that I didn't know."

Torie held on to Hunt's hand and walked to the door. "Can we stop at Willowbrook Manor? I'd like to check on Grandmama. Perhaps she'd like a ride home."

"Of course. We'll see if she's visited with His Grace long enough."

Hunt told Ethan what they were going to do and invited him to come along. He followed on his horse to Willowbrook Manor.

It didn't take them long to reach the manor, and when they did, Hunt stepped out of the carriage and reached for Torie to help her disembark.

"Have you told your father that you've purchased your bookshop?" Hunt asked.

Ethan smiled. "I don't know who was more excited when I told him I was going to sign the papers this morning and the shop would be mine—him or me."

Torie and Hunt laughed. Knowing Ethan as well as he did, Hunt was sure that he got his happy demeanor from his father.

"And Father told me he was starting to order inventory for my bookshop, especially the books that were his best sellers."

"Oh, that will be a big help—"

Suddenly, a loud gunshot stopped Hunt's words. He pushed Torie behind the carriage, where she'd be safe, then looked in the direction the shot came from.

"Ethan! Stay with Torie!"

Ethan pushed Torie to kneel behind him and shielded her with his body. Hunt pulled his gun from his jacket and fired in the direction from where the shot originated.

A barrage of gunfire came from a short distance away, and Hunt was amazed that he wasn't hit. He waited a few seconds while the shooter fired one bullet after another in his direction.

Whoever the attacker was, he wasn't a very disciplined shooter, nor was he very accurate—every shot fired went wide—but from the number of bullets, it was obvious that he had quite an arsenal at his disposal. If Hunt didn't eliminate him soon, it didn't matter how bad a shot he was. One of his bullets would eventually find its mark.

Hunt waited until he could pinpoint the shooter's location accurately, then fired his gun several times. The attacker cried out in pain, then fell to the ground.

Hunt paused long enough to make sure the gunman wasn't able to get up, then he walked to where he lay face down in the dirt and kicked the gun out of his reach.

He stared at the lifeless body, then knelt and turned the gunman over.

"Bloody hell," he whispered, looking into Connor Ralston's face.

Heavy footsteps rushed toward him and hushed voices whispered around him.

"What happened?"

"Who is it?"

"Is that Connor Ralston?"

"Is he dead?"

"Did Lord Murdock kill him?"

And then—*"Noooooooo!"*

The keening cry of Eulalia Ralston pierced the sound of the muffled voices.

"You killed him! My son!" Eulalia raised her fists and pounded

Hunt again and again, crying, "Murderer! Murderer!"

"It wasn't your fault, my lord," one of the stable hands said.

"We saw the whole thing," another Willowbrook servant said. "Ralston fired first. He was trying to kill you."

"Yes!" several other servants agreed.

It wasn't long before several men surrounded the overwrought mother and subdued her. Thankfully, her husband arrived and led her away.

Hunt pushed himself to his feet and stood on legs that threatened to give out beneath him.

Ethan stepped up beside him, clapped him on the shoulder, and pushed him through the crowd of onlookers.

Torie stepped to his other side, wrapped her arm around his waist, and walked with him inside the manor. His grandfather stood in the center of the foyer with the dowager countess. The duke stepped up to Hunt and wrapped his arms around him. He held him for several seconds, just long enough to absorb some of the shock of what had happened, then released him.

"I sent a footman for the constable," he said. "Wait in the study for him to get here before you say anything."

Hunt nodded sharply, then walked to the study. He stepped to the liquor table and poured himself a glass of whiskey. Then he sat in a chair, and Torie sat beside him. She reached for his hand and held it.

"Are you all right?" he asked her.

"I'm fine. I'm fine."

Hunt listened. He could still hear Eulalia's sobs and wailing from the courtyard. He could still see Connor's lifeless body lying in the dirt.

"You didn't have a choice, Hunt," Ethan said. "Ralston didn't give you a choice."

"I know," Hunt said, holding out his glass for Ethan to fill again.

A few moments later, Torie's grandmother rushed into the room. She went right to Torie and gave her a hug. Then she wrapped her arms around Hunt and held him for a few moments. "We are all here for you, Hunt. Your grandfather, Torie, Ethan, and me. We're all here for you."

"Thank you, my lady."

A few seconds later, the constable arrived and asked Hunt to tell him what happened. Hunt explained everything as he recalled it. Then the constable stood and excused himself.

"That's all?" Hunt asked.

"Yes, my lord. That's what the outside staff recalled, and two of the stable hands verified the same events that you did."

"What's going to happen now?"

"Nothing, as far as you are concerned. I will explain to the Ralstons that they are free to take their son home to bury him."

Hunt shook hands with the constable, and Ethan escorted him out. Jenkins opened the door and he was gone.

"Let's go home, Hunt," Torie said. "The Ralstons don't need to run into you again. We'll let His Grace take care of things here."

"Yes, you young people go on," the Duke of Willowbrook said.

"I'll stay here with His Grace and we'll call for you if anything goes awry," the dowager Countess of Wickham said.

Hunt knew they were right. The last thing he wanted was to see Eulalia or Franklin and remind them he'd just killed their son.

"I'll pull the carriage up to the garden exit," Ethan said, and left the room.

Torie gave her grandmother a hug, then Hunt escorted her to the back exit. He would be glad when he was at Wickham House and could separate himself from today's tragedy. Even though he always knew that this was how it would probably end, he hated what had happened.

When would the killing end? When would the need for money stop bringing out the worst in people? Hunt thought that when he turned his back on the war, he'd walked away from the death and destruction. But he hadn't. It still followed him.

He said a silent prayer that it was finally over.

CHAPTER TWELVE

C HRISTMAS WAS EXACTLY one week away, and the house was decorated with as much greenery as Torie could find places for. She'd strung popcorn to decorate the tree and alternated the popcorn with strings of holly berries to add color. She'd placed the tree in the red parlor and decorated it with several candles to make it glow brilliantly in the dark.

Grandmama was fearful of the tree catching fire and burning the house down, so Torie assigned one of the footmen as guardian of the tree. It was his duty to light the tree only when they would be in the red parlor, and make sure the candles were extinguished when they were out of the room.

The only things missing were the presents.

"The tree is beautiful, Torie," Grandmama told her as Torie added a few more decorations. "You must have found those decorations in the attic. I forgot I even had them."

Torie held up one of the hand-crocheted decorations shaped like snowflakes—one in red, another in green, two more in yellow, and a multitude in white. "Yes, there was a whole box of them. Did you make them?"

"Yes. I made them right after I was married. The first year I only had a few for our tree, but every year I added more and more."

"They're beautifully done, Grandmama."

"Your grandfather liked to see them on the tree. He said they reminded him of our first Christmas together."

Torie smiled. She wondered what it had been like for her grandmother on her first Christmas in her new home. What it had been like to fall in love and marry, then make memories together as you started your new life.

"Have you thought of how you'd like to celebrate Christmas, Grandmama?" Torie asked.

"Yes. I want to have Christmas here this year. I've always been alone for Christmas, and so was His Grace, so I joined him for Christmas dinner, then came home and spent the day alone. Now I have you, and Willowbrook has Hunt, so I'd like to have all of us celebrate Christmas together."

"That sounds wonderful," Torie said. "We can all go to church together Christmas Eve, then have a midnight lunch when we return home. We'll open our gifts when we wake on Christmas morning."

"Then have a large dinner later in the day and sing our favorite Christmas carols," her grandmother said.

"It will be a wonderful Christmas," Torie said. "Do you think my parents will come if I write them?"

Torie knew they wouldn't come just for her, but she hoped her father would come to see his mother at Christmas. It was long past time for the rift between mother and son to be mended.

"I doubt that he will," Grandmama answered.

"You never told me what caused the disagreement between you and Father. It must have been something important for him to have stayed away for so long."

Grandmama's face lost its smile. "Unfortunately, it wasn't all that important. But you know your father. He's very stubborn, a trait he inherits from me. We had a disagreement, something hardly worth arguing over, and he left and never returned."

"What did you argue about?"

"Actually, it was your mother."

"My mother?"

"Yes. When your father first met your mother, I knew that she was the woman he would fall in love with and eventually marry."

"They fell in love at first sight?" Torie asked.

"No, quite the opposite. They didn't seem to get along at all. But your mother was the first woman your father met who was brave enough to stand up to him. She wasn't a simpering pansy, but a sturdy rose with a few thorns."

Torie laughed. "Yes, that's Mama, all right. She can still hold her own against Father."

"Yes," the dowager countess said with a smile. "But they truly love each other. They always have."

"Then what did you and Father argue over?"

"Your father had called on your mother several times during her first Season, but he never worked up the courage to propose to her. Nor did she accept any of the suitors who offered for her. Then her second Season was turning into a repeat of her first. He would call on her regularly, but never work up the courage to propose to her. I'd finally had enough of his procrastinating. I knew if he didn't ask her to marry him soon, he would lose his chance. She was ready to marry. Anyone with eyes in their head could see that."

"What did you do, Grandmama?"

"I can't say I am proud of what I did, but I went to your grandfather and convinced him to help me. He talked to your father and told him if he didn't marry your mother, he would cut his allowance by half."

"So, you forced Father to marry Mother."

"In a way. We both know how important money is to your father. The idea of having his allowance cut in half angered him terribly. He stormed from the house and proposed to your mother that very day. His last words after they married were that he hoped we were happy, because that was the last time we would see him. And you know your father. He never goes back on his word."

Torie wanted to laugh, but the tale of her father's estrangement from his parents was too tragic to be humorous.

"I remember visiting with you when we were in Town, but now that you mention it, Father was never with us," she said.

"No. Your mother brought you and your brothers to see me regularly, but your father was never with you. The only time I heard from your father was after your scandal. He wrote to tell me about it and asked if I would consider taking you in. I wrote back immediately to tell him that of course I would take you in, and to send you immediately."

"Oh, Grandmama," Torie said, reaching out to give her grandmother a loving hug. Her grandmother hugged her back, then released her with tears in her eyes. "I don't know what I would have done if you hadn't wanted me."

"Of course I wanted you. I'd waited my whole life to have you with me."

"I'm so glad things worked out the way they did," Torie said, then rose to hang more snowflakes on the tree while her grandmother dried her eyes.

She turned from the tree when footsteps approached. It was Hunt.

"Oh my," Hunt said, entering the room. "You ladies have been quite busy this morning."

"Victoria is the one who has been busy," the dowager countess said. "I have simply been overseeing her work."

"Well, you are an excellent overseer."

"How is His Grace? Are the Ralstons still there?"

"No, they left two days ago. They took Connor's body to their home to be buried."

"Sit down," the dowager countess said, "and I'll ring for tea."

They all sat.

"Now, tell us what your grandfather had to say," Lady Wickham said. "I believe he was going to speak to Frank Ralston and express his deep sorrow."

"He told me that he had an excellent conversation with

Frank," Hunt replied. "He doesn't hold me responsible for Connor's death. He knows Connor intended to kill me. He was under no misconception concerning his son's gambling problem. That was why Fridgerton and his friend had come, so he would be first in line for the money Grandfather gave them each Christmas. He also knew he owed a man named Nixon a great deal of money, and Nixon threatened to kill him if he didn't pay it back. Frank was even afraid that Connor intended to kill his own father so he could be next for the Willowbrook title and money."

"He intended to kill you both?" the dowager countess said in shock.

"Yes, I believe those were his intentions," Hunt said.

"What kind of son would kill his own father?" Torie asked in disbelief.

"One who wanted money so badly he would do anything to get it," Hunt answered.

"Did His Grace give him the money he usually gifted them at Christmas?" Torie asked.

"Yes, I believe he did, which doesn't surprise me or disappoint me. They can use it for burial expenses, and I'm sure their income isn't that great."

"No, I'm sure it isn't. I'm glad he gave them the money, too." Torie looked at Hunt and shook her head. "I feel sorry for the Ralstons. They will never have another happy Christmas again. They'll always be reminded that this was the time of year they lost their only son."

"I know," Hunt said. "But there's nothing we could have done to change the outcome."

The dowager countess nodded and sighed. "I know you sympathize with the Ralstons, Torie, but Connor's outcome was determined a long time ago. His fate was sealed the minute he started gambling away money he didn't have. That was when his parents should have changed the direction his life was taking."

"I know, Grandmama. But it's so sad to see a young person waste his life like Connor did."

"You are too soft-hearted, sweetheart," her grandmama said, reaching for Torie's hand and holding it. "We need to be thankful for the blessings we've received in our own family."

"I am, Grandmama. I truly am. In fact, I know we could make this one of the best Christmases ever." She turned a teasing eye toward Hunt. "And it could be even better if Lord Murdock would offer to escort me to Willowbrook Village to buy some presents I've delayed deciding upon. Would you like to join us, Grandmama?"

"You two go on ahead. I think I'd like to call on His Grace. I'm sure he would appreciate a little company right now."

"I'm sure he would," Torie said with a smile. "Yes, I'm quite sure he would."

⸱⸱⸱⟫⟪⸱⸱⸱

"Where do you want to go first?" Hunt asked Torie as their carriage entered Willowbrook Village.

"I'd like to see how Ethan is coming along with his bookshop," Torie answered.

"Wonderful choice."

Hunt turned the carriage at the end of Willowbrook's main street and steered the horses down the next street. They stopped in front of the Page Turner Bookshop. "It looks like he's making progress," Hunt said, looking at the shelves already lined with books.

Hunt and Torie entered. "It's looking wonderful, Ethan," Torie said, scanning the shop.

Ethan looked up. "I wouldn't be nearly as far along if Hunt hadn't sent workers from Willowbrook Manor to help me."

"It's the least I could do. Either that or offer to help you myself," Hunt teased.

"The last thing you have is time to spend helping me unpack boxes of books."

110

"I have been a little busy helping His Grace navigate the Ralston mess."

"Is it finally over?" Ethan asked.

"Yes. Finally."

"Good."

Just then, a stranger walked through the door.

"I'm sorry," Ethan said. "I'm not open just yet."

Hunt looked at the man entering the bookshop and was impressed by his height and clean-cut good looks.

"I'll wait until you're open to buy some books," the stranger said. "For now, though, I'd like some information." He doffed his hat and laid a hand on his chest. "Forgive me. I'm Dr. James Edwards. I was looking for the Duke of Willowbrook and was told I might find his grandson here. Are one of you the man I'm looking for?"

"That would be me," Hunt said. "Have you come in answer to the advertisement we placed in the papers?"

"Yes."

"Well then, allow me to introduce myself. Hunter Melbourne, Earl of Murdock, grandson of the Duke of Willowbrook." Hunt turned to Ethan. "This is Mr. Ethan Essex, owner of this fine establishment."

"Or I will be," Ethan said, "as soon as it is open."

"Mr. Essex," the doctor replied.

"And this is Lady Victoria Crawley, granddaughter of the dowager Countess of Wickham."

"Lady Victoria," he said, bowing politely.

"Dr. Edwards."

"In the advertisement, it said that Willowbrook has a surgery set up with everything except the doctor's personal equipment. Is this correct?" Dr. Edwards asked.

"It is," Hunt replied. "Would you like to see it?"

"Very much," Dr. Edwards answered with a bright smile.

"Then allow me to take you there now. It's just down the street from here. We can walk." Hunt turned to Ethan and Torie.

"Would either of you like to join us?"

"No, thank you, my lord," Torie said. "I saw a box of stationery items. I'd love to go through them and help with the display."

"Very good. We'll return shortly."

Hunt led the way and showed Dr. Edwards to the door. "It's just at the end of this street."

They walked the short distance to the building just beyond the apothecary.

"Now that will be convenient." Dr. Edwards smiled. "A chemist directly next door. Marvelous!"

Hunt removed a key to unlock the door and led the way inside.

Since he was heir apparent to the Duke of Willowbrook, the town council members had insisted he be a member of the council. As council member, he'd received keys to all the unoccupied buildings. He would hand over the key to the new owner when the building became occupied.

Hunt stepped aside to let the doctor get a feel for the place.

Dr. Edwards stepped inside the room and gazed about. "Wonderful," he exclaimed. "Truly wonderful."

"I'm glad you approve," Hunt said. "This is the waiting room, and inside this door are five rooms. You can use them any way you see fit, but the person who planned it thought you would probably like the surgery to be the first room, the next one for medicines and supplies, and two more for whatever you need them for. But you would decide on the best use of the space."

"This is remarkable. Each patient room is complete with a bed and even equipment to treat injured patients."

"Yes," Hunt said. "And the town has set up an account at the bank with a start-up fund to pay for items we missed. It's not sizeable at the moment, but it should get you anything we've forgotten. For larger items, all you need to do is send a request to the city council. We want you to have everything you require."

"Amazing," the doctor exclaimed.

"Does that mean you're interested in applying for the position of Willowbrook's physician?"

"It does."

"I assume you have an employment history and references with you. If you would leave them with me, I'll show your papers to the council members tomorrow and let you know our decision."

"That would be wonderful. I do have one question, though. Does Willowbrook have another physician, or will I be the only one?"

"You will be the only one," Hunt replied. "Willowbrook does have a midwife who occasionally tends to other patients—mostly those with minor ailments. Is that a problem?"

"No, no," Dr. Edwards said, shaking his head. "That shouldn't be a conflict at all."

"Excellent," Hunt answered, then walked out with the doctor. "Do you have a place to stay, Dr. Edwards?"

"Yes, I've taken a room at the hotel just down the street from here, and it's very comfortable and affordable."

"Good. I'll call on you tomorrow after I've met with the council."

Hunt and the doctor parted, then Hunt walked back to Ethan's bookshop feeling confident that he'd just met Willowbrook's first doctor.

CHAPTER THIRTEEN

T HERE WERE ONLY three days until Christmas Eve, and Torie was more excited to celebrate this year than she'd been to celebrate any Christmas in her life. She felt this Christmas was going to be the most special holiday she'd ever had, though she couldn't exactly say why.

Perhaps it was because of all the decorating she'd done at Wickham House. The tree she'd decorated and strung with her grandmama's crocheted snowflakes. Or perhaps it was the evergreen boughs she'd attached to the railing on the staircase. Or the red velvet bows she'd tied to the banister. Or the smells of baking Christmas cookies and chocolates. Or any of a dozen or more other special things that heralded Christmas.

There were even presents that magically appeared beneath the tree each and every day. Torie had put a present or two under the tree herself. She only had one more present to purchase—Hunt's.

She knew what she wanted to gift him—a gold pocket watch with his name engraved on the back—but she was never alone long enough to purchase it. He was always at her side whenever she went shopping.

Finally, yesterday he'd been called to a special city council meeting to accept the new physician, Dr. James Edwards, and give an update on any new store owners who had signed leases with the bank and were opening a new business in Willowbrook Village. Ethan was among those, and Hunt wouldn't think of missing the meeting to approve his friend's new business.

Since he started filling his shelves with books, Ethan's store had been flooded with customers. Even before he opened, people had flocked from all over to see what books he had. Ethan's bookshop would be a great addition to Willowbrook, and Christmas was the perfect time to throw wide his doors.

Torie had ridden to town with Hunt, and while he was at his council meeting, she went to the gold and silver shop that Mr. Barnaby Veech had recently opened. There she had found the perfect gold pocket watch for Hunt. It came with a long gold chain, and Mr. Veech had promised to finish the engraving by today. Torie couldn't wait to see it. It would say:

HUNTER MELBOURNE
EARL OF MURDOCK
CHRISTMAS 1857
ALL MY LOVE, VICTORIA

Torie knew she was being forward with her declaration, but Hunt had told her several times over the last week that he loved her, and from the intensity of his kisses, she was sure he was going to ask her to marry him.

Torie was terribly impatient, but silently hoped Hunt would wait until Christmas Eve. That would be the most romantic time to be asked to be Hunt's bride.

She walked into Veech's Jewelry and stood at the counter admiring all the fine jewelry while Mr. Veech waited on a customer.

"Good day, my lady," he greeted her when he finished helping the customer and they were alone.

"Good day, Mr. Veech. Is my watch ready?"

"Yes, it is." He went to the back room and brought out the watch, then opened the small, narrow box. "Would you like to see it?"

"Oh, yes. Please."

He opened the box and lifted the pocket watch out. He turned it over in his hand and showed her the back.

"Oh, Mr. Veech. That is perfect." Torie's hand went to her throat. "Absolutely perfect."

"Are we expecting special news for Christmas?"

Torie felt her cheeks grow warm. "Perhaps. A girl can always hope."

"Well, congratulations. You and the earl are both extremely lucky."

"Thank you," she said.

"Allow me to wrap it for you."

"I would appreciate that," she said, then studied the jewelry items again while he wrapped her present. When he finished, Torie walked to the Page Turner Bookshop. It never hurt to have an extra present or two—just in case.

"My lady," Ethan said when she walked in. "I'll be with you in a moment."

"Take your time, Mr. Essex. I'm in no hurry."

Ethan took care of the two customers ahead of her, then came over to her when he was finished.

"I see there are several last-minute customers shopping for Christmas," Torie commented.

"Yes," Ethan said with a broad smile on his face. "This has been a very good holiday season, and books are popular items for that hard-to-shop-for person on your list."

"Oh, Ethan. I'm glad to see you doing so well."

"Thank you, Torie. I'm glad, too."

"And," she said with a smile, "I want to make sure you're coming for dinner on Christmas Eve and Christmas Day. We're planning on a big celebration."

"Yes, I'll be there. I wouldn't miss it for the world."

"Good. Now, I'd like to see your selection of romance novels. Something for Stomes, my lady's maid. Something, perhaps, by Jane Austen, or one of the Bronte sisters."

"Come over here and look," Ethan said. "My selection is getting low. I hadn't even intended to open yet, but so many people came in to get a book that I couldn't refuse them. The romance category has been extremely popular this Christmas. I don't know what there is about romance novels, but they keep growing in popularity."

"That means you haven't read any yet, Ethan, or you'd know why they are so popular."

Ethan laughed. "I'll have to put something by Jane Austen on my reading list, then."

"Yes," Torie said. "My suggestion would be to start with *Pride and Prejudice*."

"*Pride and Prejudice* it is," Ethan replied.

Just then, the door opened and Hunt entered. "I thought I would find you here," he said as he drew near to her. He placed his arm around her waist and held her close.

Torie thought she should be concerned that someone might see them standing so close to each other, but she couldn't bring herself to care. She was in love, and she wasn't concerned with who knew it.

"Are you ready to go home?" Hunt asked.

"Yes," Torie answered, "as soon as I make a purchase from Ethan."

"Oh, yes. Let me show you where to find the book you want," Ethan said.

Torie followed him to the romance section, then Ethan returned to speak with Hunt. She chose a book she was sure Stomes would enjoy, then went to the counter to pay for it. When she was done, she and Hunt bade Ethan goodbye, then went to their carriage to return to Wickham House.

"Can you believe it's almost Christmas?" Torie asked. "Only three more days."

"Torie, I have something I want to ask you."

"Is it important?"

Hunt laughed. "Well, yes. I consider it very important."

"Does it have to do with our futures?"

"Well, yes. It has to do with our futures."

"Then I don't want to hear it."

Hunt's face turned downcast. "You don't want to hear it?"

"No. I don't want to hear it right now."

"When would you like to hear it, then?"

"I'd like to hear it on Christmas Eve. If it's something you want to ask me, I want you to ask me on Christmas Eve. I want that to be the day."

Hunt wrapped his arm around her shoulders and nestled her close to him. A broad smile lit his face and launched a twinkle in his eyes. "Very well, sweetheart. I will wait until Christmas Eve to ask you this very important question."

"Thank you, Hunt," she said. She placed her head beneath Hunt's chin and took a deep, satisfying breath. Life was as close to perfect as it could be. She couldn't believe it.

It was almost like getting a Christmas miracle.

HUNT TOOK THE horses and carriage through the Wickham gate and stopped in front of the house. He held out his hand for Torie to take and assisted her to the ground.

Wilkins opened the door, and a stable hand rushed to take the horses and carriage away.

Before Hunt could escort Torie to the house, Hunt heard the loud clopping of horses' hooves and turned to see who the riders were.

"Isn't that Ethan?" Torie said.

"Yes," Hunt said, while his mind screamed that something was wrong. Ethan was waving his arms as if warning Hunt to get Torie to shelter.

"Who does he have with him?" she asked.

"I'm not sure," Hunt said, scanning the area. "It looks like

Frank Ralston. Get into the house, Torie."

"What would he be doing here?" Torie asked, just as Ethan yelled something in a frantic voice. "What did he say?" she asked, looking around.

"Get into the house, Torie. Now!"

Ethan repeated his warning, and this time Hunt heard him plain and clear. He grabbed Torie by the shoulders and tried to push her away from him. But she saw the danger the same time he did.

"No!" she screamed, and threw herself against him, wrapping her arms around his waist.

A loud shot rang out as her body crashed into his. She lifted her surprised gaze to his and came to terms with what had just happened.

"Hunt?" she said in a whisper.

"Torie!" Hunt lifted his hand from her shoulder, and it came away warm and wet. A river of blood flowed through his fingers. "No!"

Another shot echoed in the confusion, then another. But these shots came from Ethan.

"Torie! Torie, no! Dear God, no!"

"Hunt?" she said. Her voice was soft and weak and lacking any strength. A smile lifted the corners of her mouth, and she studied him as if she were memorizing his features.

"Yes, Torie. Stay with me."

"I love you."

"I know," Hunt said as tears ran down his face. "I love you too."

He gathered Torie in his arms and held her. He rocked her back and forth, back and forth. She was hurt badly, and he didn't want to move her, but he had to. He had to get her into the house.

"Pick her up," Ethan said. "Let's get her inside."

Hunt gathered her in his arms and carried her through the door and up the stairs to her room. "Stay with me, Torie. Don't leave me. Please, dear God. Don't take her away from me."

Torie's grandmother was there. So was Stomes. They removed Torie's shoes and stockings, and Hunt placed her on her stomach so he could tend to her. She'd been shot in the back. She'd taken the bullet that was intended for him.

"Has someone gone for the doctor?" he asked.

"Yes," Ethan answered. "He should be here any minute."

"Do you have scissors?" Hunt asked, and Stomes rushed over with them. Hunt cut the back of Torie's dress and pulled it open.

"Oh," Torie's grandmother cried out. "Oh, my baby."

"I need water and cloths and bandages," Hunt said, barking orders as if he were back in the army in the middle of the war.

A servant rushed in with a basin of water, and Hunt took the cloth from the water and pressed it to the wound. The bullet had gone in clean, but it was still in her flesh. He cleaned it as well as he could before the doctor arrived.

"The doctor's here," someone called from outside the room.

"Send him up," Hunt yelled. "Torie, are you still with me?"

She didn't answer, which was a good thing. If the doctor had to dig the bullet out of her flesh, it was better that she was unconscious.

Hunt heard a commotion at the door and lifted his gaze. Dr. Edwards entered the room with his black bag.

"What happened?" he asked, stepping to the bed.

"She was shot."

Hunt watched as the doctor did all the things he was expected to do. He cleaned the wound with a disinfectant, then poured a generous amount of alcohol in and around the wound. He soaked a cloth in the alcohol and cleaned the area around the wound a second time, then reached in his bag and took out a long, pointed tool similar to scissors, but with a flat head. He poured more alcohol in a pan and placed the instruments he intended to use in the alcohol, then he looked up at Hunt.

"I need you to hold her still."

Hunt nodded, then placed his hands on one side of Torie.

Ethan placed his hands on her other side.

"Ready?"

The doctor pressed the instrument inside the bloody wound and searched for the bullet. She screamed in pain.

Hunt whispered in her ear. "I'm right here, sweetheart. Stay with me. I'll take care of you."

The scissors slid from the wound, not having found the bullet. Dr. Edwards re-inserted the instrument and twisted it, searching.

Torie cried out in agony again and again. Each time, Hunt felt like lashing out at the world for inflicting this cruelty on a complete innocent. He felt helpless to take away her pain. All he could do was pray that his touch might reassure her that she was not alone.

He was scarcely able to watch as Edwards dug for the bullet, and his relief was palpable when this time the instrument slid from the wound with the bullet gripped tightly in its jaws. Edwards dropped it into a metal pan, letting it hit the bottom with a metallic clink. He reached for the alcohol and washed out the place where the bullet had entered her flesh.

Hunt looked at her. Her face had lost all color and she had no strength. For the first time, he realized how close he was to losing her.

What would he do if she died? How would he survive if she wasn't with him, wasn't in his life?

"Stay with me, sweetheart. You can't leave me. I won't survive if you do."

Dr. Edwards worked steadily to clean her wound and bandage it. She wasn't conscious. Hunt wasn't sure what was worse, hearing her in so much pain, or seeing her unconscious and so close to death.

"I'm right here, sweetheart. It's over now. You need to be strong. I need you, Torie. I need you to be with me."

Dr. Edwards finished with the bandaging and gently laid a clean sheet over her. His care and concern for his patient showed in every movement. When he was done, he looked at Hunt. "What happened?" he asked.

"She took the bullet that was intended for me."

"Then you're lucky she did. It would have struck you right in the gut. Those are the most painful wounds, and usually the most fatal."

"Will she be all right?" Hunt asked. He needed a little reassurance. Just enough to continue living without giving up.

"I can't tell you she will. She lost a lot of blood. Her chances aren't good."

Hunt's eyes filled with tears, and they streamed down his face. He didn't even try to stop them. It would do no good. They ran in rivers.

"What can we do?" Hunt asked. He'd do anything to make her live.

"Pray," Dr. Edwards said. "That's the only thing left. She's in God's hands now. And pray that she doesn't get a fever. That's the last thing she needs to fight off."

CHAPTER FOURTEEN

D R. EDWARDS WAS finishing taking care of Torie and restoring his instruments to a ready state. Hunt could only watch as each of them disappeared into the doctor's black bag.

"Why don't you go to the drawing room and tell the dowager countess what we know?" Edwards said. "The more prayers going up to God, the more they will be heard. Then you can come back up to stay with Lady Victoria. She'll need to be watched closely for the next thirty-six hours."

Hunt left the room, and Ethan followed. "How were you able to come so quickly?" Hunt asked as they walked down the stairs.

"Just plain good timing, I suppose. Frank Ralston found me at the bookshop right after you left. He wanted to know if I'd seen his wife. He was frantically looking for her. I said I hadn't seen her, and he muttered something like *that means she's gone after him*. I asked who she'd gone after, and he told me Hunter Murdock."

"She blames me for her son's death."

"He was so sure she was going to do you harm that we rode out as fast as we could. But we didn't get here in time."

They reached the bottom of the stairs and went to the room where the dowager countess waited for word concerning her granddaughter.

She looked so small and fragile sitting there. Thankfully, she wasn't alone. Wilkins was with her, as were several maids and footmen, keeping vigil.

"Is she still alive?" she asked.

"Yes, my lady," Hunt said. "But her injury is severe. Dr. Edwards believes her life is in God's hands now."

The dowager countess' eyes filled with tears. Slowly, they spilled down her cheeks.

"Would you like His Grace to be with you? I know he would like to know what's happened to Victoria."

"Yes, I would like that very much," she said.

"Wilkins, would you send someone for His Grace?"

"Right away, my lord," the butler said. Wilkins left the room and gave the instructions to one of the footmen.

"I need to know, Lord Murdock," Lady Wickham said. "What happened? How did this come about? Is it true that Eulalia shot Victoria?"

"Yes, my lady. This is all my fault."

The dowager countess focused a harsh look on Hunt. "Do not even think that, Hunter. None of this is your fault. None of it."

"But it is. If I hadn't killed Connor—"

"He would have killed you," she countered. "He would have *killed* you. Then he would have killed your grandfather. Then his father would have inherited the Willowbrook dukedom and all the Willowbrook wealth. Then Connor would have gambled away everything your grandfather worked to build. And Torie would have died alone and lonely. And…" She stopped. "Need I continue?"

"No, my lady. You have explained the error in my thinking clearly enough. I see where your granddaughter gets her ability to reason things out."

"Yes. Our minds tend to work similarly."

Hunt stood and poured a glass of brandy for himself and Ethan, and a glass of wine for the dowager. He handed her the wine, then Ethan his brandy, then he sat on the sofa opposite the dowager. He lifted his glass but stopped before it reached his lips.

"How will I survive if Torie dies?"

"Torie will not die," Lady Wickham said. "She is not meant to die. Not yet."

Hunt closed his eyes and let the wetness trapped behind his eyelids spill down his cheeks. He took a swallow of his brandy, then stood. "I must get back to Torie."

Ethan stood too. "I need to get back to the village. I left the bookshop unattended."

Wilkins came into the room and announced that footmen from Wickham Place had gone to collect the Duke of Willowbrook, and he should be here at any time.

Ethan walked out of the room with Hunt. "Will you return when you close your shop?" Hunt asked his friend.

"Yes. I'll be back."

Hunt made his way to Torie's room and walked to the bed. He knelt at Torie's side and took her hand in his. "Has she awakened yet?" he asked Dr. Edwards.

"No, nor do I expect her to. I gave her a liberal amount of laudanum in some wine. She should sleep for a good while yet." The doctor packed his bag and walked toward the door. "I'll return later tonight. Keep putting cool cloths on her neck and back, and watch for a fever. If she stirs, give her more of the laudanum in wine. That should keep her as still as possible. We don't want her wound to start bleeding again."

"Thank you, Dr. Edwards. I appreciate everything you've done. I just…I just thank God you've come to Willowbrook."

"Take care of yourself, Lord Murdock. The family can't afford for you to get ill, too."

"I'll be fine," Hunt said, then watched Dr. Edwards leave the room.

Stomes was quietly attending her mistress, and she stepped around the bed to pick up the basin. "I'm going to get some fresh water," she said. "Do you need anything, my lord?"

"No, I just want to be alone with Torie for a while."

"Very good. I'll be back later, then," she said, and left the room.

The love of his life lay on her stomach with her face turned toward him. Her glorious golden hair cascaded to the side, her face far too pale against the sheets. Hunt stroked the silky blonde tendrils, smoothing them back and away from her face. She was so very lovely. His fingers moved tenderly across her cheek, then drifted down her jawline to her chin, and he allowed his thumb to trace her lips.

"I love you, Torie. I don't think I told you how much I love you. If I did, I didn't tell you often enough."

He reached for her hand and brought her fingers to his lips to kiss them. "Do you know, I never thought I would fall in love. I always knew I would marry, but I never thought it would be for love. I didn't believe in love. I thought that was an emotion meant for people like my grandfather and your grandmother. Never for me. And then you entered my life." Hunt smiled. "No, you *saved* my life. You found me in that cold cottage and brought me here and healed me. And I realized it was possible for me to love. You were my angel, and I'd fallen in love with you."

Hunt kissed her fingers again, then swiped at the tears that spilled from his eyes and ran down his cheeks. Through the tears, he looked at her and gently touched her cheeks. "Don't leave me, Torie," he whispered. "Please, fight to stay with me. I can't lose you. I'd only be half a man without you."

Hunt held her hand and continued to speak to her. He wanted her to know that he loved her and that he was here for her. He wet a cloth in clean, fresh water and held it to her lips. She needed the moisture.

After a while, Stomes returned. She offered to sit with Torie so he could leave for a few minutes, but Hunt wouldn't leave her. The thought of her slipping away while he was gone was too terrifying for him to contemplate.

The hours went by. The sun slowly faded, then went away completely. Stars shone in the sky as if it were a night like every other night, but it wasn't. This night was different. Desperately different.

A little later, Ethan returned.

"What have you heard about Frank Ralston?" Hunt asked, mostly to have something to talk about. He didn't care about anything except for Torie—and he especially didn't care about the woman who had shot her.

"Eulalia's dead, you know," Ethan said.

"No, I didn't know. Who killed her?"

"I did," Ethan confessed. "She had just fired her gun and looked as if she would fire again, so I stopped her. I'm just sorry I couldn't stop her before she shot Victoria."

Hunt looked at Ethan. "Thank you," he said. "I know I shouldn't be glad, but I am. She was aiming for me. But Torie stepped in front of me to protect me."

"I know," Ethan said. "She's one very brave lady."

Tears spilled from Hunt's eyes again. "I wish she hadn't done it. I'm stronger. I should have protected her."

"You can remind her of that when she's recovered," Ethan said, and Hunt smiled at the humor in his statement.

Ethan filled a glass with brandy and gave it to Hunt. Together, they sat and talked for a while longer, then Ethan went down to sit with the dowager countess and the Duke of Willowbrook. Torie's grandmother and Hunt's grandfather climbed the stairs several times to check on Torie, but they didn't stay long. Hunt knew it was too difficult for them to see her as injured as she was. Too difficult for them to see her as close to death as she was.

Finally, Dr. Edwards returned. He checked Torie's wound and changed her bandage. With persistence, he managed to get her to drink a little more wine with laudanum and felt her forehead.

"She's warmer than she was earlier. Keep putting cold cloths on her." He showed Hunt where to place the cold cloths for the best effect.

Stomes assigned two maids to set water outside in the cold so it came close to freezing. Then she would bring it up to the room. But no matter how diligent they were, the ice-water cloths seemed to be in vain.

A few hours after midnight, Torie began to shift on the bed. Her arms flailed and her feet pounded the mattress. She bent her knees and shuffled as if she were trying to climb or run.

"No, Torie. Stay still," Hunt whispered, but she continued to thrash.

He placed his hand on her forehead but knew before he touched her that she would be burning up. And she was.

"Help me, Stomes. Hold her steady."

Torie's maid ran to the opposite side of the bed and held her mistress as steady as she could while Hunt held her tightly from his side. Hunt was startled by her strength, and that she fought them as vigorously as she did.

"Go down and get Ethan," he ordered Stomes, and she ran from the room.

A few seconds later, Ethan entered. He knew immediately what Hunt needed and went to the opposite side of the bed to keep Torie from thrashing. While he and Ethan held her, Stomes put cloths in the icy water and placed them on Torie's neck and every other place Dr. Edwards had instructed Hunt to place them.

While they were still fighting with Torie, the dowager countess entered the room with His Grace close behind her.

"How is she?" she asked, rushing to her granddaughter's side and trying to comfort her.

"She's developed a fever," Hunt answered.

"Do you think I should write her parents? They will want to know," she said in a thick voice. "They may want to see her before…if…"

Hunt held on to Torie. Everything inside him screamed no. He didn't want to admit that it was time to contact her parents because she was close to death. And yet it was obvious that she was.

"Yes, my lady. Contact them. Tell them to hurry."

The Duke of Willowbrook placed a steadying hand on the dowager countess, then led her from the room.

With tears in his eyes, Hunt leaned down and whispered in Torie's ear. "Don't you leave me, Torie. Don't you dare. I love you too much to lose you. I love you."

AFTER WHAT SEEMED like hours, Torie finally lay still.

Hunt didn't know what was worse, watching her fight for her life—at least he knew then that she was still alive—or watching her lie still as death. And not knowing if it had claimed her.

Hours later, her skin cooled and her fever broke.

"Torie?" he whispered.

Her eyelids fluttered and tried to stay open, but failed.

"Oh, Torie. You're back." Hunt looked to Ethan. "She's better, Ethan. She's going to be all right."

"Yes, Hunt," Ethan said with a smile on his face.

"Can I get you anything? What do you need, Torie?"

"Water," she said in a weak, raspy voice.

Hunt poured some water into a glass, then he and Ethan shifted her enough that she could drink. It was difficult, being careful not to open the wound on her back, but they managed to get a little water into her.

"I'm going to go tell Victoria's grandmother the fever has broken," Ethan said. "She'll be very relieved."

Ethan left, and Hunt reached for Torie's hand. She tried to open her eyes again but they continued to flutter shut. She fell asleep shortly after, and stayed asleep.

By midmorning, Hunt was still in the chair beside her bed when the door opened and the dowager countess entered with two people close behind her. Hunt rose.

"Lord Murdock," the dowager countess said. "Allow me to

introduce my son Anthony, Earl of Wickham, and his wife, Lady Eloise."

"Lord and Lady Wickham, it's a pleasure to meet you," Hunt said.

The pair looked to where their daughter lay on the bed. Tears streamed down Lady Wickham's face.

"Oh, Victoria," she said, and stepped around her husband to kneel at Torie's side.

"Has she regained consciousness?" the earl asked.

"For a few seconds, then she fell asleep again," Hunt replied. "But her fever seems to have broken."

"That is a good sign, is it not?" Torie's father asked.

"Yes, my lord. A very good sign."

The dowager countess staggered and reached out to steady herself against the poster of the bed. Her son reached for her and led her to the cushioned chair.

"Sit down, Mother. You've spent too much time awake. His Grace said you've been keeping a vigil all night. You must take care of yourself."

"I know, Anthony. I'm not getting any younger."

"You're not that old, Mother. But I shouldn't have stayed away so long."

"And I shouldn't have kept you at arm's length like I did. It was so silly of me."

"Of both of us."

The dowager countess reached up and clasped her son's hand.

"Come, Mother. Let me take you to your room. You need to rest for a little while."

The dowager countess stood, then let her son lead her from the room. "You will wake me if Torie rouses, won't you?"

"Of course," Hunt said. "I'll come and get you myself."

The door closed behind them, and the younger Lady Wickham smiled with tears in her eyes. "I've been waiting nearly thirty years for that to happen. It's only too bad it took Victoria almost dying to bring it to pass."

Hunt looked at Torie lying on the bed and wished she'd been awake to see it. It was the miracle she'd always hoped would happen.

CHAPTER FIFTEEN

ORIE SLOWLY OPENED her eyes and tried to look around the room, but since she was lying facedown on the bed, it was quite difficult to see anything. She tried to lift herself up enough to see more of the room, but a searing pain shot through her back to her shoulder.

She lowered her head again and took in several deep breaths until the pain subsided, then tried again. This time she could keep her eyes open long enough to see Hunt. He was slumped in the chair snoring softly. He looked pale and exhausted. She wondered how long he'd been there. She wondered how long *she'd* been here. How long it had been since she was shot.

Torie watched him for a little while, absorbing the growth of stubble on his face. She had to admit that she liked the look of him with some facial hair. It made him appear more rugged and handsome, if that were possible. Almost piratical. And his hair was mussed in an attractive way. She wondered how long it had been since he'd combed it.

Torie shifted her gaze to the window. The sun was shining, so it wasn't night. That meant she'd slept at least one night. She wondered how much longer.

She turned her attention back to where Hunt slept. She wanted to let him sleep, but if she did, she'd never find out how long she herself had been sleeping, and what had happened to Eulalia

Ralston. Plus, she was terribly thirsty, and she'd never get anything to drink if she didn't wake the poor fellow up.

"Hunt," she whispered.

He didn't move.

"Hunt," she whispered a little louder.

Nothing.

She cleared her throat, then said, "Hunt," louder still.

Hunt moved, then jerked awake. "Torie?" He pushed himself up in the chair and leaned toward her. "Torie! Oh, Torie!" He reached for her hand and held it to his lips.

"How do you feel?" he asked, then laughed.

"Like I've been…shot," she answered.

"Oh, that was a dumb question, wasn't it?"

"Yes, but I don't mind. It was good to hear your voice."

"Would you like something? Water? Food?"

"Water, Hunt."

"Of course." He rose and poured some water into a glass, then stood over her. "It's going to hurt when I move you," he said.

"I know," she replied.

He rolled her to her side, then lifted her head and brought the glass to her mouth.

Torie moaned when he moved her, then had to stop to catch her breath until the pain lessened. When she was ready, she drank from the glass. "Thank you," she said.

Hunt lowered her onto the bed and placed several pillows where she requested them to make her more comfortable.

"Now, what else can I get you?" he asked.

"Nothing. Sit down and tell me what I've missed. Everything. How long was I asleep?"

Hunt sat in the chair and took her hand in his. "You've been asleep for four days."

"Four days? That means today is…"

"Christmas Day. It's a good thing you woke up today, or you would have missed Christmas altogether."

"Oh, and I was so looking forward to it."

"It's still early. There's still a lot of this Christmas Day left."

"Yes. There is." Torie stopped to catch her breath. "What happened to Eulalia?" she asked when she could breathe again.

"She's dead."

"Dead? How?"

"Ethan had to do it. He had no choice. He saw her the same time you did and shot her, but he wasn't in time to stop her before she fired at us."

"I couldn't believe it when I saw her point her gun at you. Do you think she's the one who killed your brother? Or—"

"It doesn't matter, Torie. It's over now. We're all safe."

"Is your grandfather here?"

"My grandfather is here. Dr. Edwards is here. He came to check on you, and your grandmother invited him to stay for dinner. Ethan is here. And," he said with a grin, "your mother and father and brothers are here."

"My family is here?"

Tears sprang to her eyes, but these were tears of joy. "Will you take me to see them, Hunt? I want to see my family all together."

Just then, Stomes came into the room. "You're just in time, Stomes," Hunt said. "Your mistress insists that she wants to go down to surprise her family. Would you get her a dressing gown?"

"Of course."

Stomes went to the wardrobe and took out Torie's best robe. She and Hunter took great care in helping Torie into it. Then Stomes combed and styled Torie's hair. When she was done, Hunt picked Torie up in his arms, and Stomes put a lap robe over her.

"Your family is going to be very surprised, my lady," the maid said.

"Yes, Stomes," Torie replied. "I feel as if I've been given a Christmas miracle."

Hunt carried her out of the room and walked down the stairs with her in his arms. When they reached the room where Torie had decorated the tree, Stomes stepped inside the door and called for everyone's attention.

"In honor of the season, I have a special Christmas miracle I know you will all enjoy," she said. "Merry Christmas!"

Stomes threw the door wide and stepped aside as Hunt walked through the open doorway with Torie in his arms. The somber, quiet room rang with riotous cheers and applause. Everyone surrounded her and wanted to give her a loving embrace, but Hunt refused to let them touch her for fear they would hurt her back and shoulder.

He lowered her to one of the cushioned chairs and gave her parents and grandmother room to join her.

Hunt met Torie's brothers for the first time, and was impressed with their physical attributes as well as by their mental acumen.

"Lord Murdock," Torie's older brother said, stepping up to Hunt. "Allow me to introduce myself. I am Richard Crawley, Viscount Beldon, Torie's older brother, and this is Torie's younger brother, Winston. On behalf of my family, I'd like to thank you for everything you've done for Victoria."

"I thank you," Hunt answered, "but I have to make it plain that it was because of me that your sister was shot and almost died."

Richard and Winston laughed. "If you think you can take any blame for Torie stepping in front of you to take that bullet in your place, you are sadly mistaken," Richard said. "Saving people is in her nature. Her attempt to save Frances Bradley from her husband is what caused Father to send her from London in the first place. Stepping in to save people is what she does." He chuckled and scratched an eyebrow. "There's a dog running around one of Father's estates enjoying a life of freedom because Victoria saw that he was being abused by his owner and she couldn't stand to have him chained up with little to eat or drink.

She claimed she rescued him, but when Father saw him roaming around in our home, he realized that she'd stolen him. Father knew that the only way he could save Torie from being charged with thievery was to take the dog to the country and let him live in the stables. That was several years ago, and the dog is still enjoying his freedom."

"Yes, that sounds like something Torie would do," Hunt agreed.

"Yes, so don't think you can blame yourself for her effort to save you. You are just one of several pets she's saved."

Hunt laughed. "I guess I am. One of her pets."

"Although you must be very special to her," Richard said.

"What makes you say that?"

"Just a look she gets when you look her way. I'm sure it's nothing important."

"Perhaps not," Hunt replied. "So, have you been to town to see the progress Willowbrook is making? Have you noticed how it's grown?"

"Yes. Win and I spent several hours touring your town yesterday afternoon. Quite impressive."

Hunt noticed the hesitation in Torie's brother's words. "Quite impressive except—what?"

"One thing Win and I noticed as we were investigating your town is that there are no businesses devoted to the male clientele."

"Businesses such as what?" Hunt asked.

"Such as the sparring establishment similar to the one Gentleman Jack runs in London," Win chimed in.

"Or a gambling house," Richard said, before listing several other businesses that were absent. "And there's also a need for a gentlemen's club and a—"

"Richard," Torie said in a voice that stopped her brother's words. "That's enough. Hunt can only do so much. He's waiting for investors to open up different shops."

"Would you consider accepting my application for an establishment?" Win said.

Hunt smiled. "I would. For anything except a brothel. That is the one establishment the city council has decreed is inappropriate in Willowbrook."

"I see," Win said. But there was something in the tone of his voice and the look on his face that warned Hunt there could be trouble in the offing. "But you would consider a gentlemen's club?"

"The city council would have to discuss it and vote on it."

"Interesting," Winston said.

"Are you saying you would consider being in the working class? That's not exactly what is expected of the son of an earl."

"No, I wouldn't work in the establishment. I'd hire someone to run it." Torie's brother sat back with a grin on his face. "My only job would be to smoke my cigar and collect the profits."

Hunt smiled at Torie's brother. These were the ramblings of a man who had never worked a day in his life. Hunt wondered how he'd get along in the real world.

After a while, Dr. Edwards suggest that Torie had been up long enough and needed to go back to bed. Hunt carried her to her room, and the doctor followed them. He changed her bandages, then gave her a little wine laced with laudanum, and as expected, she soon fell asleep.

Hunt watched her for a while, then excused himself when Torie's mother came up to relieve him for dinner. Torie's father accompanied his wife and stepped into the room to check on his daughter.

"We had a close call here, didn't we?" the Earl of Wickham said with tears in his eyes.

"Yes, we did, my lord," Hunt said. "Too close. May we never have to go through anything like this again."

"She's a special lady, don't you think?"

"Yes, my lord. She is very special."

"Perhaps you'd like to enlighten me as to your intentions, Lord Murdock."

"I would," Hunt said. "I intended to make a trip to London to speak to you, but with all that's gone on, I haven't been able to. I intend to marry your daughter."

"Have you spoken to my daughter yet?"

Hunt could not hide his broad smile. "Oh, yes, my lord. As you know, your daughter has her opinions on marriage, and has openly voiced them."

The Earl of Wickham turned to look at his wife, and they broke out in easy laughter. "Yes, Lord Murdock. I am well aware of my daughter's views. And has she agreed to your proposal?"

"Yes, my lord. Wholeheartedly. But she wanted me to wait until Christmas Eve to issue my proposal. And she would give me her answer on Christmas Day. She thought it would be more special that way."

"Yes, she would," Lady Wickham agreed with tears in her eyes.

"Well then," Torie's father said, "I'll let you work out the details. Just know you have my approval. My complete and unconditional approval."

"Thank you, my lord," Hunt replied.

"I will let you gentlemen go down to have lunch with the rest of the family," Lady Wickham said, "and I will stay here with our daughter. It has been far too long since I've last seen her. Now, go along. And before you return, Lord Murdock, you might wish to catch a bit of a nap. You look as if you've missed several days of rest."

"Yes, my lady," Hunt said, then he and his future father-in-law left the room and went down to join the rest of his new family.

TORIE HADN'T THOUGHT it possible to sleep as long as she had, not after the days she'd already slept since she was shot. But when she opened her eyes, the sun was a distant memory and darkness blanketed her room.

Hunt was still in the chair beside her, like he'd been the entire time she had struggled to recover. She wasn't sure if he'd left her for even a moment, but he must have, because he looked as though he'd bathed and put on fresh clothes. He had a bit more color to his face, and the deep worry lines had faded at least a little.

She watched him sleep for a few more minutes and enjoyed watching him. No one had the right to be this handsome. No one had the right to be this perfect. How had she ever been fortunate enough for him to fall in love with her? How had she been lucky enough for him to want her as badly as she wanted him?

Then, as if he realized she was watching him, he opened his eyes and looked at her.

"Did you wake up?" he asked in a sleepy voice.

"Yes, finally," she answered. "Why did you let me sleep so long?"

"Because you needed the rest," he said. "How do you feel?"

"Much better. I hardly hurt at all."

"That's good. Just make sure you don't overdo it."

"I won't," she replied.

"What?" he asked when she fell silent. He could tell she was thinking, and that it was serious.

"Is it still Christmas?"

He looked at the clock on the mantel. "Yes. There's about an hour left until it's over."

"I have something I want to give you."

"You do?"

"Yes, I do."

"And I have something I want to give you, too. And a question I want to ask you."

"Then you'd better hurry and ask it," she said. "We're running out of time."

Hunt reached for her hand and held it, then knelt on the floor beside her bed. "Torie," he said in a soft, emotional voice. "I love you. More than I thought it was possible to love anyone."

"And I love you too," she said.

"I know you do. You've told me you do, and if I had any doubts, they've disappeared. You stepped in front of me and would have given your life to save me. That's the truest form of love. To be willing to give your life to save mine."

Hunt reached in his pocket and took out the little box she'd seen before.

"Victoria Crawley, would you do me the honor of becoming my wife?" he asked, then slipped an engagement ring on her finger.

"Of course I will, Hunter Murdock. I knew the moment I found you half dead in old man Jackson's cottage that you were the man I wanted to marry and spend the rest of my life with."

"You did?"

"Of course I did. A woman always knows these things."

"How did you know?"

"Because you sent shivers racing up and down my spine when I touched you."

"No I didn't."

"Yes, you did. That's when I knew I was going to marry you."

Hunt leaned over her and pressed his lips to hers. "I wish you had told me then."

"I couldn't," she said. "You had to figure that out on your own."

"There's a lot I should have figured out that I missed," Hunt said.

"Don't worry," she teased. "You'll have a whole lifetime to figure things out."

Hunt kissed her again, then stretched out on the bed beside her and held her.

"Merry Christmas," he wished her.

"Merry Christmas," she wished him back. With her smile still in place, Torie fell into blissful sleep.

CHAPTER SIXTEEN

TORIE HAD BEEN confined to her bed for nearly a week before Dr. Edwards gave her permission to spend at least part of the day out of it, and she made use of every minute. She dressed, then went down to the morning room to visit with her mother and father and two brothers, who were still at Wickham House.

Dr. Edwards had returned to Willowbrook to take care of the growing number of patients who wanted to see him. Ethan returned to his bookshop to continue to stock his shelves with the books his father had sent from London to be added to his inventory. So the only people left at Wickham House were the members of Torie's immediate family, her grandmother, the Duke of Willowbrook, and Hunt.

"Mama," Torie said one afternoon when they were all seated in the library, enjoying a relaxing afternoon. "Hunt and I would like to get married. Hunt's already spoken to Papa and received his approval. He has even secured a special license. There's nothing to prevent us from marrying. As long as you are all here, I would like to marry as soon as possible."

Her mama's eyes grew big. "Are you sure you don't want to get married in London?"

"Quite sure. I want the ceremony here, with all of you with me."

Her mother looked at her husband, and he nodded with a

smile on his face.

"I suppose that would be agreeable," she answered. "As long as it's all right with your grandmother."

"Grandmama?" Torie asked.

"There's nothing I would love more," her grandmother answered.

"Very well then," Torie's mother said. "When would you like to have the wedding?"

Torie turned her head and locked gazes with Hunt. He simply smiled at her, and that was answer enough.

"Tomorrow," she said.

"Tomorrow?" her mother and father both exclaimed in surprise.

"Yes, tomorrow," she said. "There's no sense in spending time doing nothing when we could be married and getting on with our lives."

"Do you see what kind of a female you're marrying, Lord Murdock?" Richard said, and everyone laughed.

"Oh, yes," Hunt replied. "I am well aware of how impulsive she is. She impulsively jumped in front of a bullet to save me and nearly got herself killed. Let's just hope her next impulsive movements don't have such dire results."

"I couldn't agree more," her father said. "So, if you are aware of her shortcomings, her mother and I might as well approve of your decision to marry immediately." Lord Wickham turned to his mother. "Can your cook handle preparing a wedding breakfast on such short notice?" he asked his mother.

"That will not be a problem," the dowager countess told her son. "My cook is a miracle worker."

"Very well," the younger Lady Wickham said. "Tomorrow it is. The only part you will have to take care of is contacting the vicar. Can you do that, Lord Murdock?"

"I can," Hunt assured them. "I've already informed him to be prepared for a wedding without much notice."

"Very well, then. Tomorrow it is," the Earl of Wickham said

amid a rousing round of applause.

Hunt turned to Torie and kissed her.

"I can't wait until we're married," he whispered.

"I can't wait until I'm healed," Torie replied in a breathy whisper.

THE NEXT MORNING, Torie woke and got out of bed with a smile on her face. This was her wedding day. The day she would take Hunt as her husband, and he would take her as his wife. This was a day she'd sometimes thought would never come. But it had. That day was now.

Torie bathed then dressed in the gown she'd chosen for the ceremony. When she was dressed and her hair was styled, she walked down the stairs and into the drawing room on her father's arm.

She took the first step toward the man she was going to marry and paused. She didn't pause because she was hesitant to get married to Hunt. She paused because if she didn't slow down, she'd run the rest of the way to him. This was the happiest day of her life. This was the day she would become the Earl of Murdock's wife.

The vicar performed the ceremony, and Hunt repeated the words he was supposed to say. Torie only had to be prompted once or twice. Not because she wasn't sure of what she was supposed to say, but because she was concentrating so intently on the man she would spend the rest of her life with that she couldn't concentrate on the words.

Finally, the vicar asked her if she would take Hunt to be her lawfully wedded husband, and she answered yes with tears in her eyes. Her heart wanted to burst inside her when the vicar asked Hunt if he would take her to be his lawfully wedded wife, and he lowered his gaze to look her in the eyes and said, "Oh, yes.

Forever."

Then the vicar pronounced them husband and wife.

Everyone in the room burst into applause, and Hunt leaned in to kiss her.

She'd never been so happy in her entire life. Never thought her life would be so perfect. But it was. And would be.

Forever and ever.

EPILOGUE

TORIE OPENED HER eyes and looked at the man lying next to her. Her body warmed and her heart swelled in her breast. They had been married more than two months already, and every day seemed as miraculous as the first day had been.

They made their home at Willowbrook Manor, partly because this would be where they would eventually live, and as long as the Duke of Willowbrook was alive, they would be close at hand to watch over him. Although that wasn't the all-consuming job it might have been if the Duke of Willowbrook and the dowager Countess of Wickham hadn't shocked everyone to pieces when they announced that they intended to marry. But that turned out well.

After His Grace and Torie's grandmother married, Torie's father, the Earl of Wickham, decided to make Wickham Place his country estate. He privately told Torie that he'd been estranged from his mother far too long over something so insignificant that he could hardly remember what it was. So Torie had her family close around her, and Hunt's grandfather, too. She couldn't have been happier.

"Are you going to sleep all day?" she asked when she turned her head to see Hunt watching her.

"I might be tempted to as long as I have such a perfect view."

Torie laughed, then leaned over to give her husband a quick

kiss. "Well, I'm afraid your view is going to be changing. I have to get up and get busy. I promised Grandmama that I'd take her to Willowbrook Village to do some shopping."

"What does she intend to buy?" Hunt asked on a laugh. "She only has to mention an interest in something and my grandfather sends a footman to buy it. I can't imagine anything she might need that she doesn't already have."

"Well, she mentioned a need for some yarn."

"Yarn? What does she need to make with yarn?"

Torie tried to keep her expression from changing. "She mentioned she wanted to get started on some baby things."

"Baby things? For whom?"

"I'm not sure, but I think she mentioned something about herself."

"Herself!"

Torie laughed. "Well, not *for* herself, but for her to give away. As gifts."

"Oh," Hunt said. "You scared me for a moment. I'm not an expert on women's matters, but I didn't think women your grandmother's age had children any longer."

"They don't, but Grandmama is making things for her granddaughter."

"Oh," Hunt said, then stopped. "I didn't know she had another granddaughter besides you."

"She doesn't."

"That means…"

"Yes. That means she's crocheting some baby clothes for me."

Hunt turned to face her. "Are you saying that you're going to have a baby, Torie?"

"Someday," she answered.

"But not now," Hunt said. He raked his fingers through her hair. "Bloody hell, Torie. You frightened me."

"Are you frightened to have a baby?" she asked.

"No, I'm not frightened for me, but I'm terrified to think of you going through that."

"Why? Women have babies all the time."

"I know, but…"

"But?"

"I'm not sure I'm ready to be a father yet."

"When do you think you'll be ready?"

"I don't know. Maybe in a couple of years."

Torie tipped her head back and laughed. "Well, Hunt. I'm not sure I can give you that long."

"Why? How long do you think we should wait."

"I think you only have about six or seven months."

Hunt stared at her with eyes as big as saucers. "You're pregnant now! Now! How could you be pregnant already?"

"Didn't your grandfather tell you how it happens?"

"Well, of course he told me, but I didn't think it could happen already."

"Oh," Torie said, wanting to laugh at him. "You thought we had to practice longer until you got it right?"

"No, I didn't think we had to practice longer. I'm obviously a quick learner. I just thought…"

"Are you happy, Hunt?"

He stopped. "Of course I'm happy." Hunt wrapped his arms around her and cradled her next to him. "I'm very happy. Very."

"Good," Torie said, then placed her head beneath his chin and let him hold her.

"How many children do you anticipate us having, Torie?"

"I hadn't really thought about it," she answered. "I guess that depends on how avidly we intend to practice." Torie wrapped her hand around the nape of his neck and brought his head down so his lips met hers.

"Do you think we should practice now?" he said, kissing her again.

"Well, it's already too late to worry that you might get me pregnant," she teased, and he pushed her back against the bed as he came over her.

"Then we might as well spend the day practicing," he said, and kissed her again.

About the Author

Laura Landon taught high school for ten years before leaving the classroom to open her own ice-cream shop. As much as she loved serving up sundaes and malts from behind the counter, she closed up shop after penning her first novel. Now she spends nearly every waking minute writing, guiding her heroes and heroines to find their happily ever afters.

She is the author of more than a dozen historical novels, including SILENT REVENGE, INTIMATE DECEPTION, and her newest Montlake Romance release, INTIMATE SURREN-DER.

Her books are enjoyed by readers around the world.

www.ingramcontent.com/pod-product-compliance
Lightning Source LLC
Chambersburg PA
CBHW071939190726
48293CB00004B/1285